CRYSTAL FIGHTERS™

DARK HORSE BOOKS

CRYSTAL FIGHTERS™

CREATED, ART, & STORY BY

JEN & TYLER BARTEL

President & Publisher MIKE RICHARDSON

Collection Editor DANIEL CHABON

Assistant Editor BRETT ISRAEL

Designer BRENNAN THOME

Digital Art Technician ALLYSON HALLER

This volume collects the digital comic series *Chaos Arena: Crystal Fighters*, originally edited by Jim Gibbons and published by Stela.

Library of Congress Cataloging-in-Publication Data

Names: Bartel, Jen, author, artist. | Bartel, Tyler, author, artist.
Title: Crystal fighters / Jen and Tyler Bartel.
Description: First edition. | Milwaukie, OR : Dark Horse Books, August 2018.
| Summary: Stella is a bored teen who plays in a seemingly positive all-ages virtual reality called "Crystal Fighters," but she soon discovers a dark side to the game where other players have created a secret magical girl fight club.
Identifiers: LCCN 2018009540 | ISBN 9781506707952 (paperback)
Subjects: LCSH: Graphic novels. | CYAC: Graphic novels | Virtual reality--Fiction. | BISAC: JUVENILE FICTION / Comics & Graphic Novels / Superheroes. | JUVENILE FICTION / Comics & Graphic Novels / General.
Classification: LCC PZ7.7.B375 Cr 2018 | DDC 741.5/973--dc23
LC record available at https://lccn.loc.gov/2018009540

Published by
Dark Horse Books
A division of Dark Horse Comics, Inc.
10956 SE Main Street
Milwaukie, OR 97222

DarkHorse.com

To find a comics shop in your area, visit comicshoplocator.com

First edition: August 2018
ISBN 978-1-50670-795-2

1 3 5 7 9 10 8 6 4 2
Printed in China

Chaos Arena

CRYSTAL FIGHTERS

RADIO. TELEVISION. PERSONAL COMPUTERS.

EACH GENERATION IS DEFINED BY A TECHNOLOGY THAT SHAPES THE YOUNG AND FRIGHTENS THE OLD. FOR MY GENERATION, IT'S ***VIRTUAL REALITY***.

WITH SIMULATIONS INDISTINGUISHABLE FROM REAL LIFE, YOU'D THINK HUMANITY WOULD ENTER A NEW ERA OF ENLIGHTENMENT. INSTEAD, I GET...

CRYSTAL FIGHTERS™

BY JEN & TYLER BARTEL

NOT FOR GIR-- ARE YOU SERIOUS?!
WHY DIDN'T YOU JUST GET ME *STAY-AT-HOME BAKER* OR *FUTURE BRIDE-TO-BE*?

REALLY, STELLA?
DO YOU *HAVE* TO CHALLENGE EVERYTHING?

JUST TRY IT, STELLA!
THE SALESPERSON TOLD US IT'S REALLY POPULAR WITH GIRLS YOUR AGE.

AUNT KELLY SAID JESSICA LOVES IT!
THAT'S 'CAUSE JESSICA'S **BASIC**.

~SIGH~
ALL RIGHT... I'M GONNA GO CHECK IT OUT.
THANKS, GUYS.
I'M SURE IT WILL BE FUN.
IT WON'T BE.

DAD'S RIGHT--*CRYSTAL FIGHTERS* IS REALLY POPULAR WITH GIRLS RIGHT NOW.
BUT WHY DO I ONLY GET TO PLAY STUFF THAT'S POPULAR WITH GIRLS?

WHAT'S WRONG WITH A GIRL ENJOYING A LITTLE...

...CARNAGE?

OH WELL. I GUESS FOR NOW, THIS IS THE CLOSEST I GET.
MAYBE I'LL FIND SOME WAY TO MAKE THIS STUPID GAME FUN.

STELLA
KIM
LEVEL 4
HP 235
MP 57
EXP 603CP
LVL UP 310CP

WELCOME TO CRYSTAL FIGHTERS! ENJOY YOUR GAME!
OMG STELL??
UGH. COUSIN JESSICA.
STELLLLLLLS!!!
I DIDN'T KNOW YOU PLAYED THIS GAME!!?
I MEAN, IT'S MY FIRST TIME.
I'M NOT EVEN SURE WHAT I'M DOING...
...

NO WAAAAAAYYY LOL!!!
LET ME EXPLAIN THE RULES!!!

JESSICA'S GUIDE TO CRYSTAL FIGHTERS

CRYSTAL FIGHTERS SHOULD ALWAYS LOOK PRETTY!

NEW USERS RECEIVE A STANDARD UNIFORM, BUT YOU CAN FIND MORE OUTFITS IN THE GIFT SHOP!

COLLECT CRYSTAL POINTS TO BUY THEM OR WHINE TO YOUR PARENTS UNTIL THEY GIVE YOU THEIR CREDIT CARD! *~TEE-HEE~*

CRYSTAL FIGHTERS *NEVER* HARM THEIR ENEMIES.

INSTEAD, WE CONVERT THEM TO FRIENDS USING OUR UNWAVERING RESOLVE AND A PURE HEART! CONVERT ANYONE THAT LOOKS UNPLEASANT INTO A FRIEND!!

WITH EACH NEW FRIEND, YOU'LL CHARGE YOUR CRYSTAL BROOCH!

THE POWER OF A CRYSTAL FIGHTER COMES DIRECTLY FROM THIS ITEM!! WITH EACH CHARGE, YOUR ABILITIES INCREASE AND ADDITIONAL PARTS OF THE GAME WORLD OPEN!

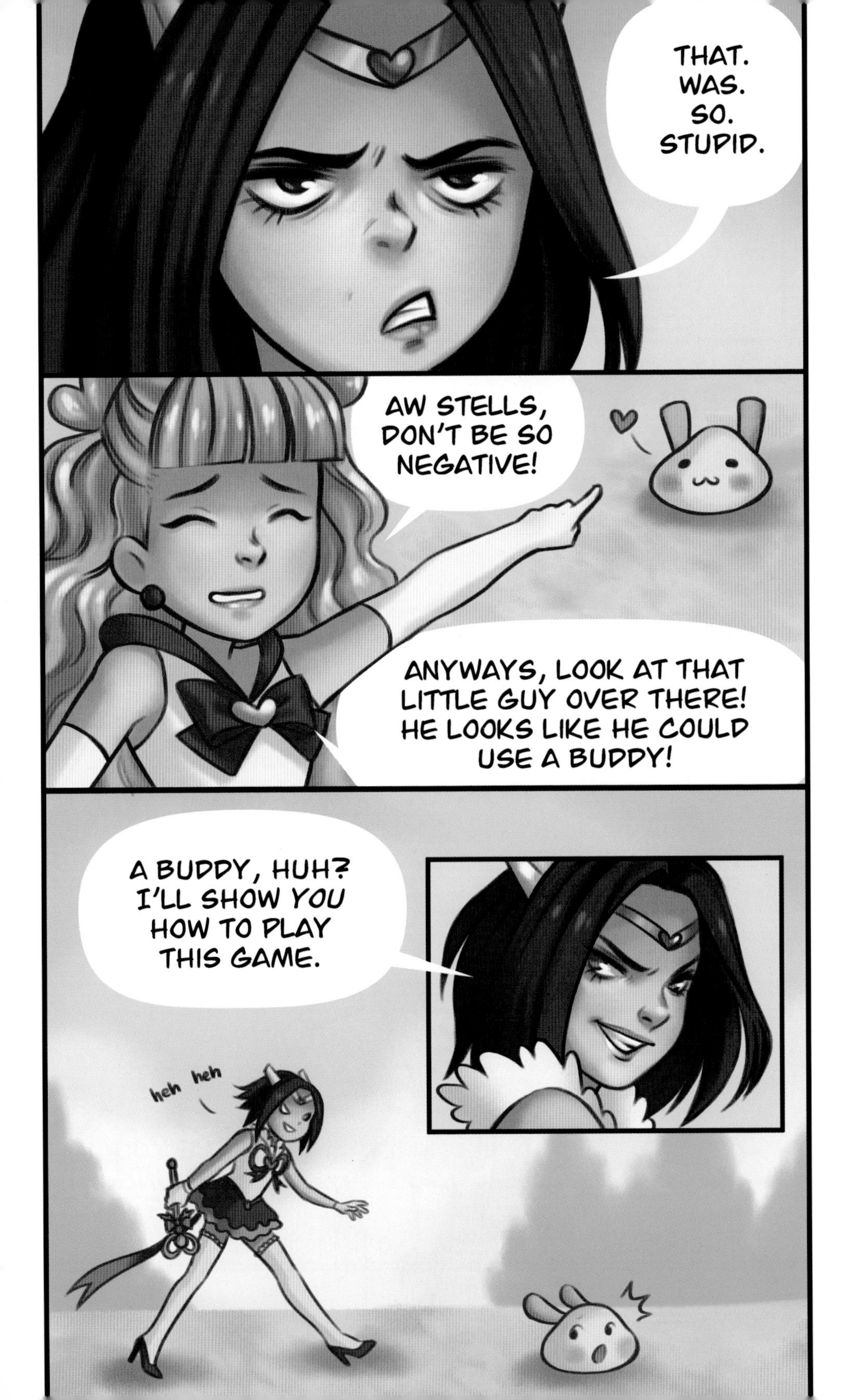
THAT. WAS. SO. STUPID.
AW STELLS, DON'T BE SO NEGATIVE!
ANYWAYS, LOOK AT THAT LITTLE GUY OVER THERE! HE LOOKS LIKE HE COULD USE A BUDDY!
A BUDDY, HUH? I'LL SHOW *YOU* HOW TO PLAY THIS GAME.
heh heh

I'M SORRY, YOU ARE IN VIOLATION OF THE **CRYSTAL FIGHTERS** TERMS OF AGREEMENT! IMPROPER USAGE OF YOUR WAND WILL RESULT IN A **FIFTEEN-MINUTE TIME-OUT.**

WHOA. THAT WAS WEIRD.
I'M DONE WITH THIS GAME! I'M DONE WITH *YOU!* I'M DONE WITH ***LIFE!***
STELL, WAIT!!
I HAVEN'T EVEN TOLD YOU ABOUT ***THE CRYSTAL PRINCE*** YOU CAN DATE!

OMG I CAN'T EVEN RUN AWAY FROM YOU BECAUSE I'M WEARING *HIGH HEELS!!!*

WHAT KIND OF FIGHTER WEARS HIGH HEELS?!!

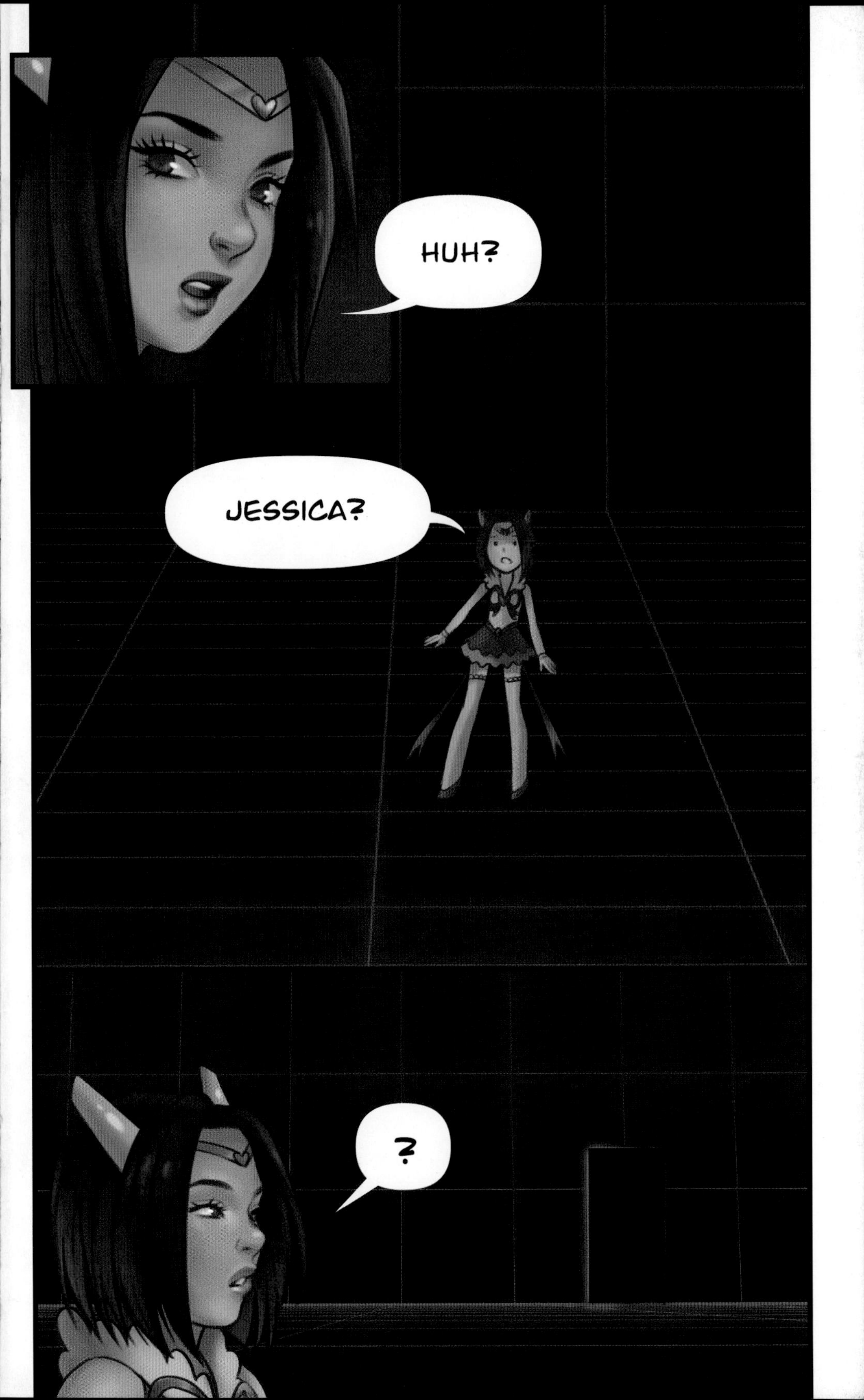
HUH?
JESSICA?
?

SHAAAA

LET THE CHAOS BEGIN!

WHIIISSSH

Glek!

YAAAAAHHHHHHH
AM I...?
THESE GIRLS ARE NOT WEARING APPROVED OUTFITS.
NO F ! WAY!
OR USING APPROVED LANGUAGE.

AND THAT IS DEFINITELY NOT AN APPROVED WAY OF MAKING FRIENDS.

FWWEEEEWW
shOOOOOO
KR
KU

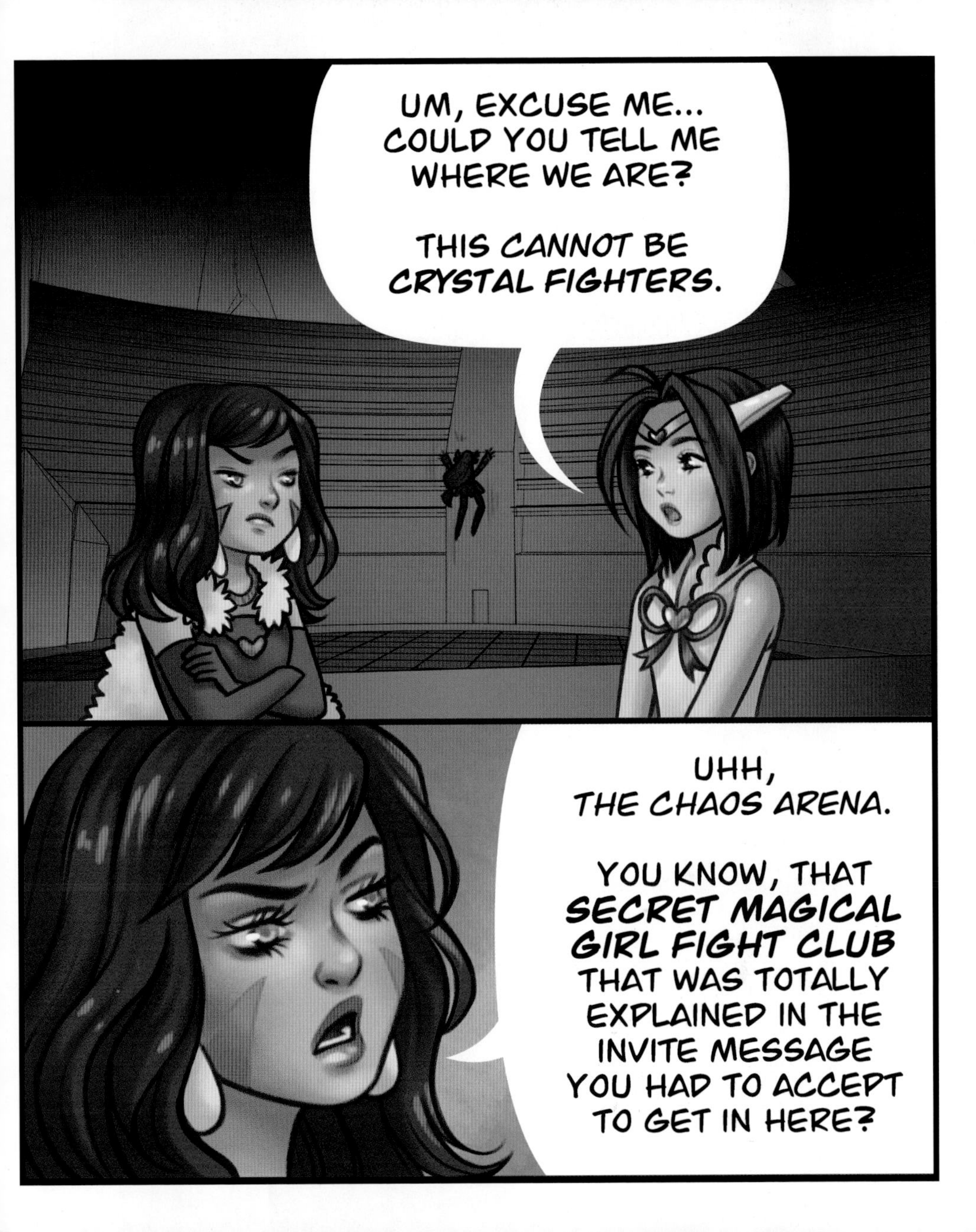
UM, EXCUSE ME... COULD YOU TELL ME WHERE WE ARE?
THIS CANNOT BE CRYSTAL FIGHTERS.
UHH, THE CHAOS ARENA.
YOU KNOW, THAT SECRET MAGICAL GIRL FIGHT CLUB THAT WAS TOTALLY EXPLAINED IN THE INVITE MESSAGE YOU HAD TO ACCEPT TO GET IN HERE?

MAGICAL GIRL... FIGHT CLUB...

SO YOU REALLY DIDN'T READ THE INVITE, HUH?

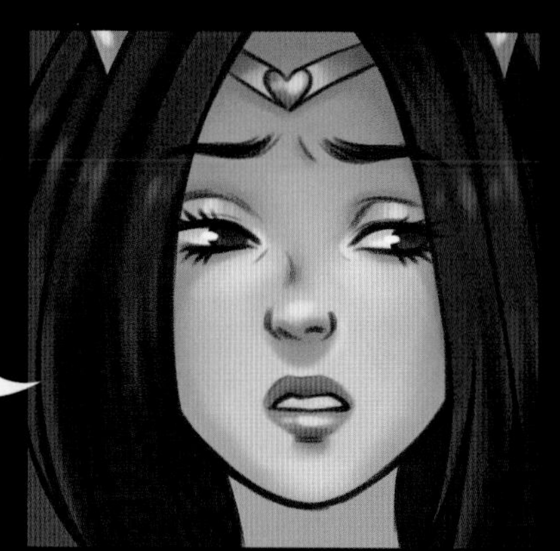
I MEAN, I DIDN'T EVEN GET ONE.
I WAS PLAYING CRYSTAL FIGHTERS AND I GOT SUPER ANGRY AT MY STUPID COUSIN AND THEN THE GAME GOT GLITCHY AND--

WAIT, YOU WEREN'T INVITED HERE?!
huff
huff

YOU'RE GONNA PAY FOR THAT CHEAP SHOT!

SPECIAL ATTACK
WRATH OF THE
DIVINITY PRISM

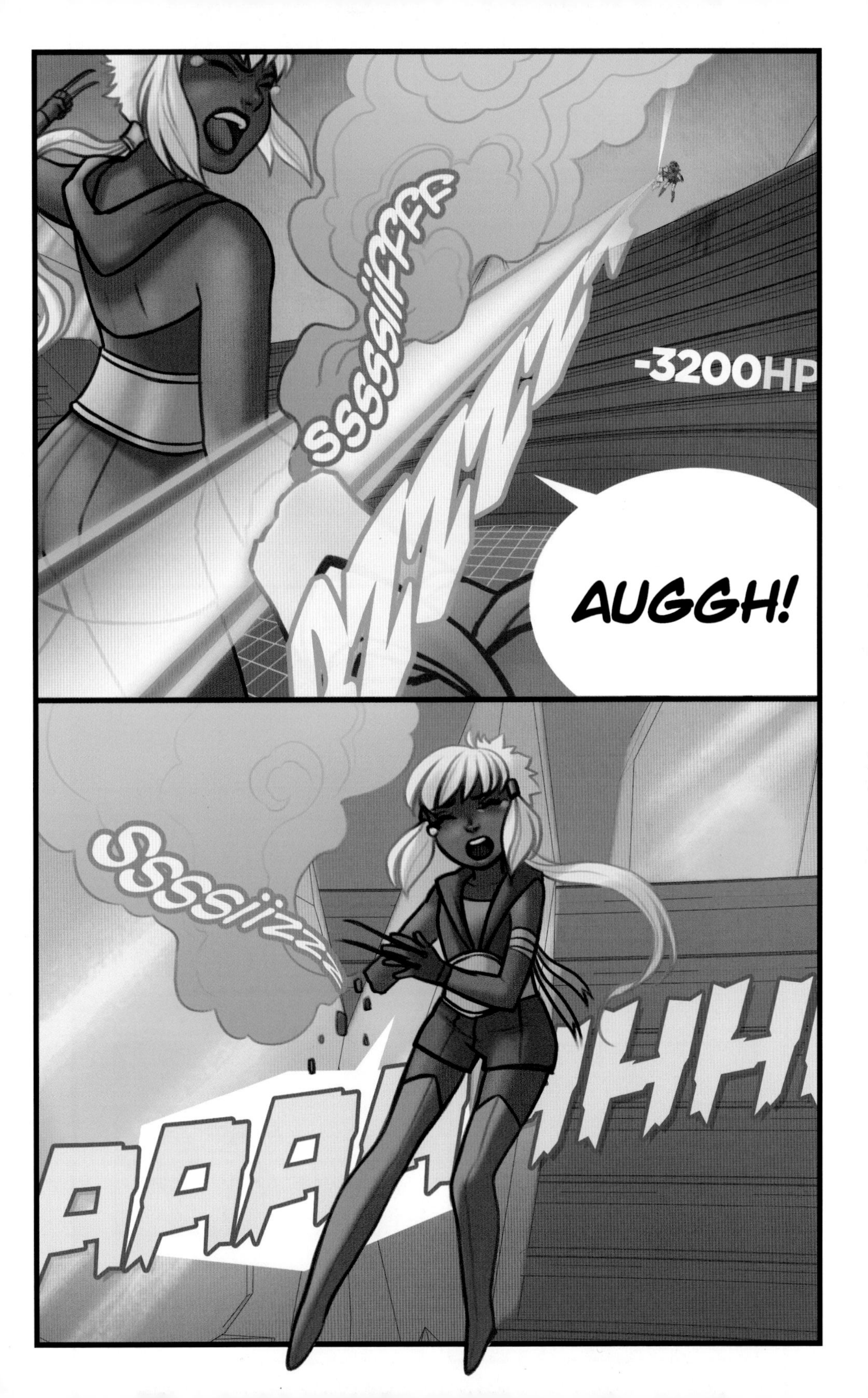
SSSSSIIFFF
-3200HP
AUGGH!
SSSSIIZZZZ
AAAAHHHH

ECCHHRK
SHOOOOO
tsh

!

O SILENT SENTRY WHO DWELLS BENEATH, DORMANT AND ALL-SEEING: HEED MY CALL...
FFSSSSS

SPECIAL ATTACK

CHTHONIC FIST

KUUUUU

-3200HP
PRKOW

heh
heh

VICTORY: EGYPT

REWARD FOR VICTORY
+2 Levels (New Level: 23)
+1367 Crystal Points
New Item Prism Tiara

PENALTY FOR DEFEAT
-2 Levels (New Level: 20)
Battle Ban 12 hours

STRONGEST SINGLE ATTACK:
Wrath of the Divinity Prism
-3200HP

SPECTATORS' RATING:

JEEZ, HOW DID THIS EVEN HAPPEN?
I THOUGHT YOU COULD ONLY ENTER WITH A KEY!
I SUGGEST YOU LEAVE BEFORE PENELOPE FINDS OUT!

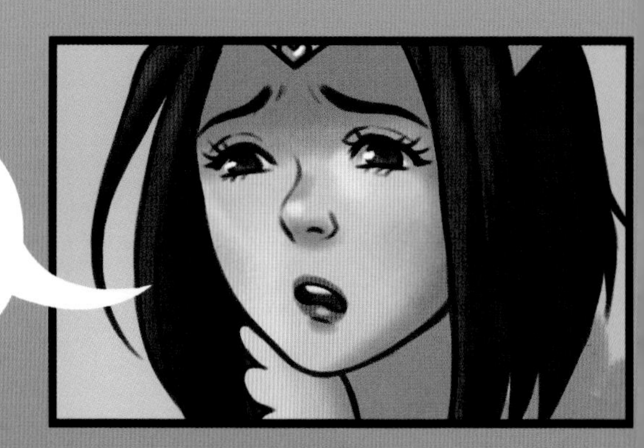
LOOK, THIS IS ALL A MISUNDERSTANDING. I--

WHAT PART OF GET OUT DO YOU NOT UNDERSTAND?!
YOU AREN'T WANTED HERE. GO. NOW.

FINE!

GOD, IF THEY SHUT THIS PLACE DOWN, I DON'T KNOW WHAT I'M GOING TO DO.
NO WAY, MAN. THE CHAOS CLUB AREN'T AMATEURS--THEY'D NEVER LET THE COMPANY FIND OUT ABOUT THIS PLACE.
THIS SERVER USES 4096-BIT ENCRYPTION ROUTED THROUGH AN ONION NET OVER THE DARK WEB.

DUDE, YOU TOTALLY JUST SAID A BUNCH OF THINGS THAT YOU THOUGHT SOUNDED SMART.

HEY, NEW GIRL!
YOU CATCH THAT? THIS PLACE USES STATE-OF-THE-ART ENCRYPTION! WITHOUT A KEY, YOU DON'T COME BACK.

WHATEVER.
ME BEING HERE IS A MISTAKE ANYWAY...

THE CHAOS CLUB DOESN'T MAKE MISTAKES. IF YOU'RE HERE, IT WAS NO ACCIDENT...
... AND YOU'RE GOING TO PROVE IT TO EVERYONE BY STEPPING INTO THE RING!

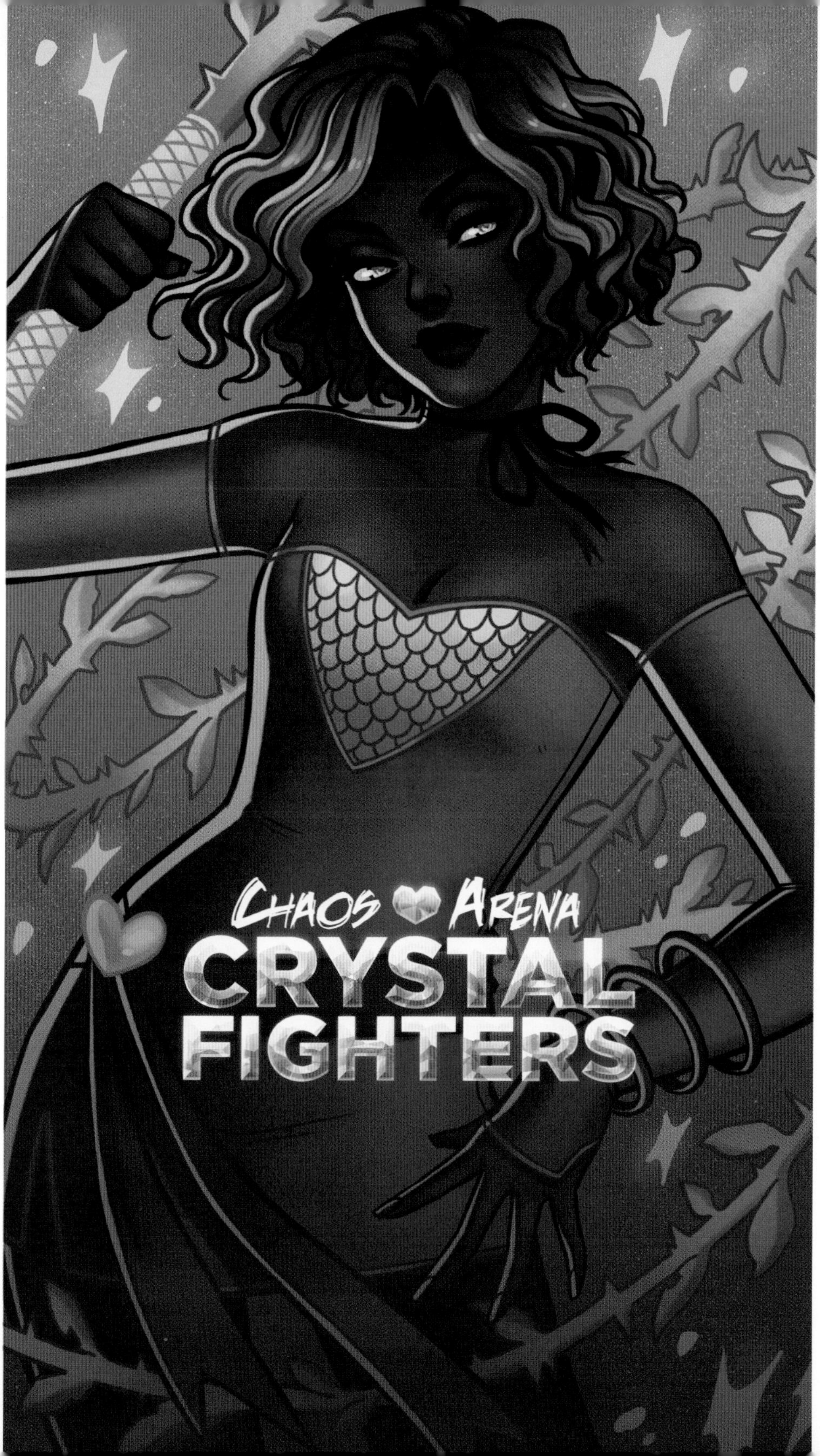

Chaos Arena

CRYSTAL FIGHTERS

HEY!
I'M HOME!

MOM?
Olive—
working late
tonight, left some
cash for dinner.
love,
mom
FIGURES.

HAPPY BIRTHDAY TO ME, I GUESS.

OLIVIA
JONES
LEVEL 22
HP 3466
MP 1807
EXP 5988CP
LVL UP 650CP

SHE READY YET, DOC?
IF ONLY.
WE MADE IT THROUGH THE BASICS, BUT SHE'S SPENT THE LAST NINETY MINUTES CREATING A CUSTOM OUTFIT.

FINDING SOMETHING THAT WORKS WITH HER ABNORMALLY SIZED HEAD HAS BEEN... CHALLENGING.
DOO DOO
LOOKIN' SUPER COOL

TA-DAH!
WELL? HOW DO I LOOK?
HOW YOU LOOK ISN'T GOING TO MATTER MUCH WHEN YOU'RE GETTING YOUR TEETH KICKED IN.

DOC SHOWED ME THE ROPES. I'M PRETTY CONFIDENT WITH SPELLS AND ITEMS.
GOOD. SO WHICH WEAPON DID YOU CHOOSE?

YOU'RE LOOKIN' AT 'EM.

A BRAWLER, HUH?
WELL, LET'S SEE IT! SHOW ME HOW YOU THROW A PUNCH!

EH!

THAT WAS--AN' I'M NOT JUST SAYING THIS--THE WORST PUNCH I'VE EVER SEEN.
WELL, I'VE NEVER ACTUALLY PUNCHED SOMETHING BEFORE...
OKAY, OKAY. NOBODY'S BORN AN EXPERT. I'LL GIFT YOU SOME OF MY CRYSTAL POINTS SO YOU CAN LEVEL UP YOUR STATS.
LEVEL UP
STRENGTH STRENGTH STRENGTH STRENGTH STRENGTH
STR
INT
VIT
LUK
AGI
THAT'S NOT HOW--
AND MORE STRENGTH.

SINCE YOU USED YOUR CRYSTAL POINTS IN THE WORST WAY POSSIBLE...
...TAKE THESE GLOVES. THEY'LL HELP BALANCE OUT YOUR STATS.
GO AHEAD, TRY THEM ON.
NEW ITEM ACQUIRED
ATHENIAN GAUNTLETS
All stats receive +20% of highest stat value
One-time revival after TKO.

NOW THIS I CAN GET USED TO.
THEY'LL GIVE YOU A ONE-TIME REVIVAL IF YOU GET KNOCKED OUT IN BATTLE...
...THOUGH YOU SHOULDN'T BE IN ANY HURRY TO GET YOURSELF KILLED.
HEY, OLIVIA...
WHY ARE YOU DOING THIS FOR ME?

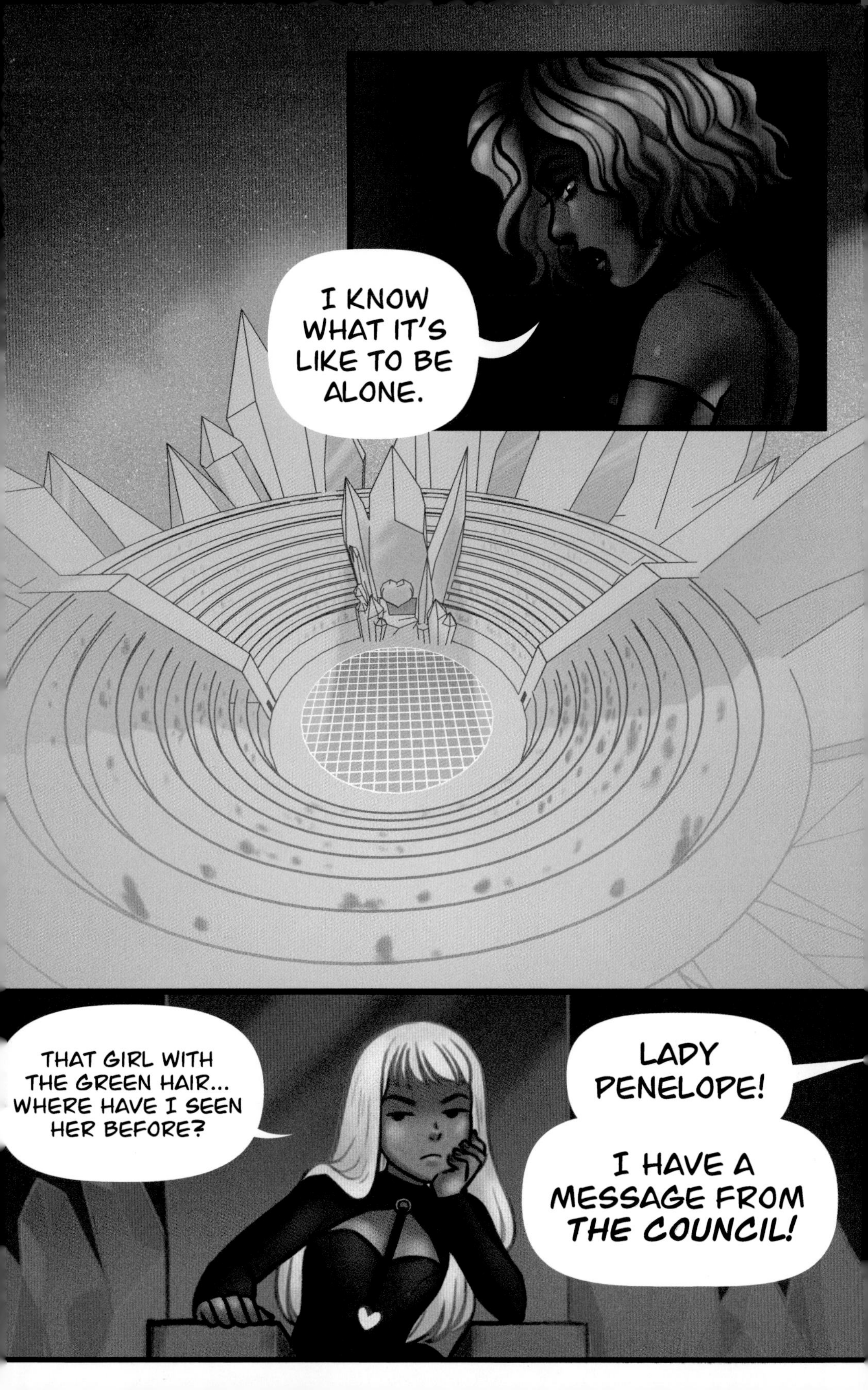
I KNOW WHAT IT'S LIKE TO BE ALONE.
THAT GIRL WITH THE GREEN HAIR... WHERE HAVE I SEEN HER BEFORE?
LADY PENELOPE!
I HAVE A MESSAGE FROM THE COUNCIL!

2vs2 BATTLE:
OLIVIA
STELLA
SERAPHINA
ELEKTRA

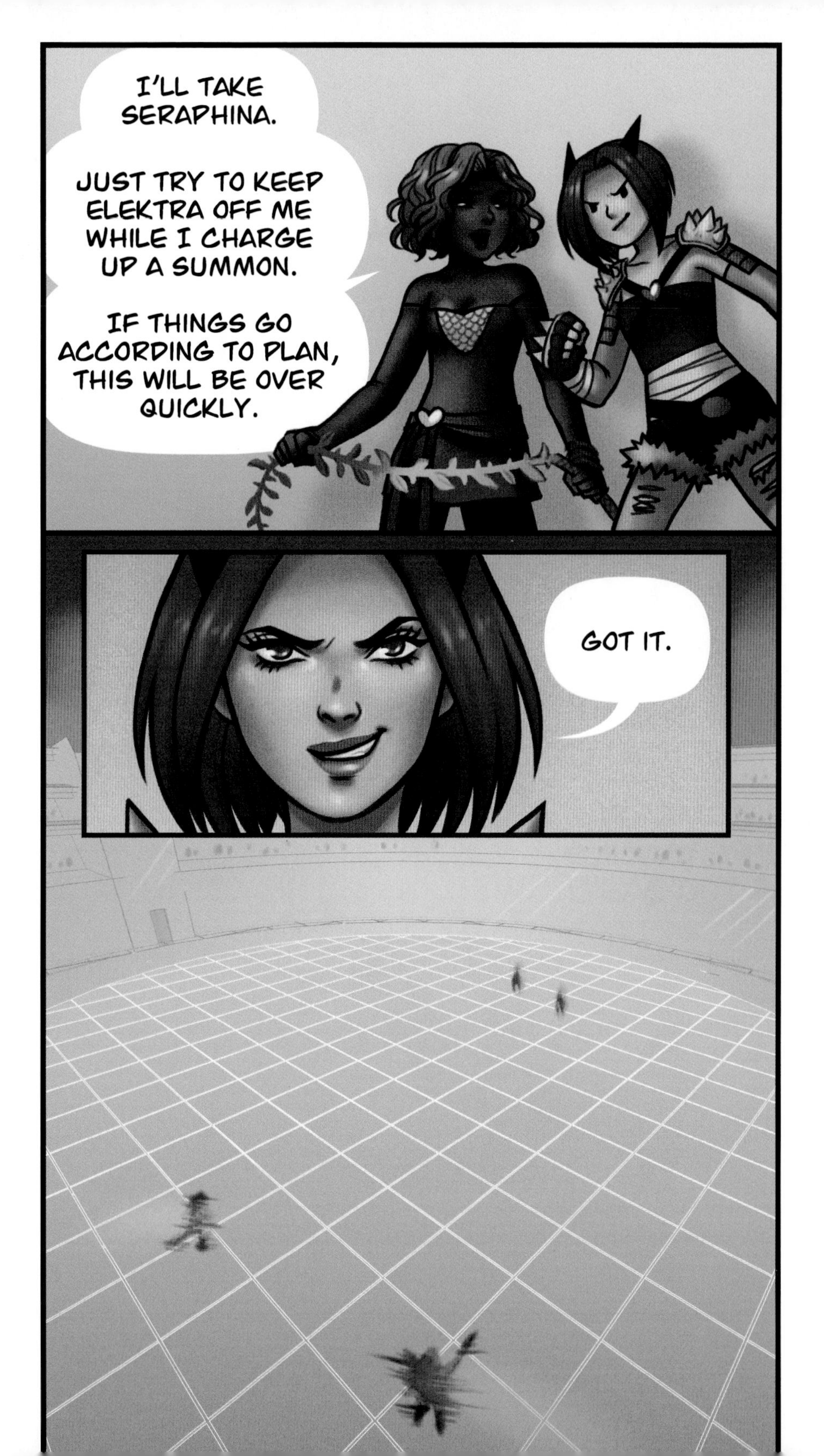
I'LL TAKE SERAPHINA.
JUST TRY TO KEEP ELEKTRA OFF ME WHILE I CHARGE UP A SUMMON.
IF THINGS GO ACCORDING TO PLAN, THIS WILL BE OVER QUICKLY.
GOT IT.

shooooof
shiiish
WHOA.
THEY'RE MOVING SO FAST I CAN BARELY SEE THEM!
OH COME ON, YOU'RE MAKING THIS TOO EASY!

ZZZAAT
THUNCK

ZURRAAAGG
OLIVI--
AHHH!!

HANG IN THERE!

SHOOOOFF

THWAK
AUUGGHH!
WHO PUNCHES SOMEONE IN THEIR EAR?!

NOW, NOW, THAT WASN'T VERY NICE.
I THINK YOU NEED TO BE TAUGHT A LESSON.
!
GET BACK, STELLA!

SUMMON CHARGED

CRYSTAL SUMMON

DECACORN: THE TEN-HORNED BUTCHER

WHOAAAA...

shyewwww

whissh

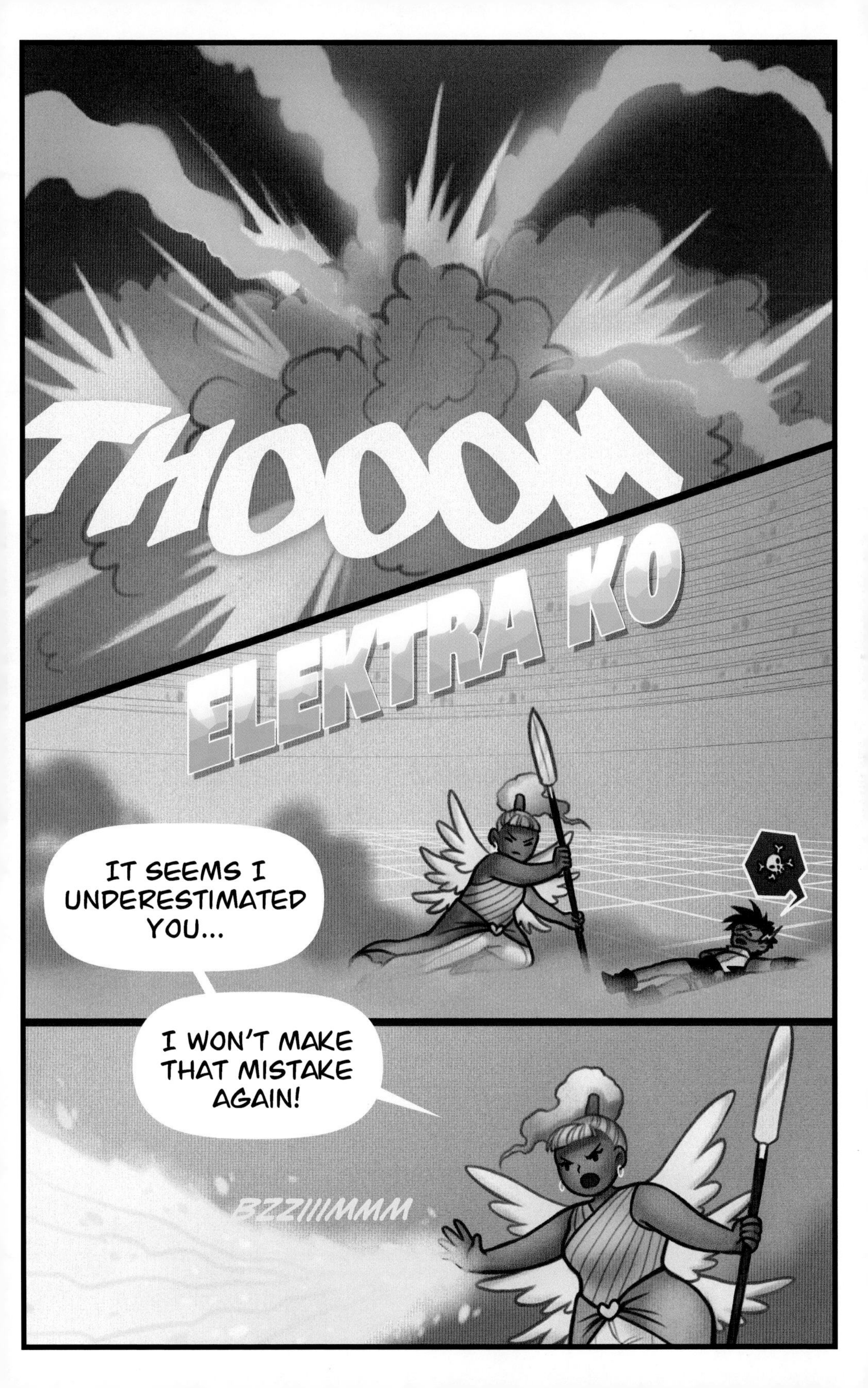
THOOOM
ELEKTRA KO
IT SEEMS I UNDERESTIMATED YOU...
I WON'T MAKE THAT MISTAKE AGAIN!
BZZIIIMMM

AHHHH!!!

...ERGGH...

DON'T YOU TOUCH HER!

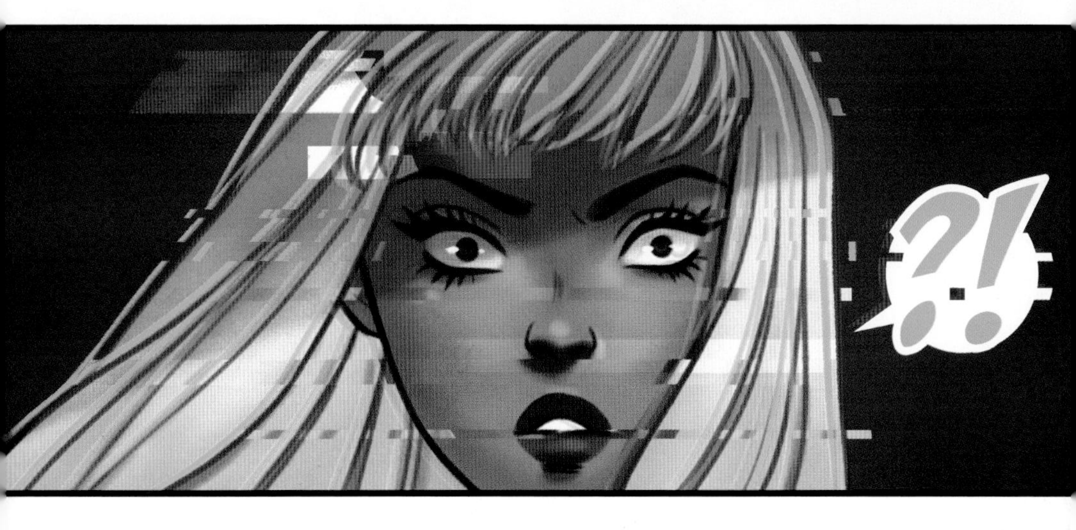
?!

Kunk

WUUHHH

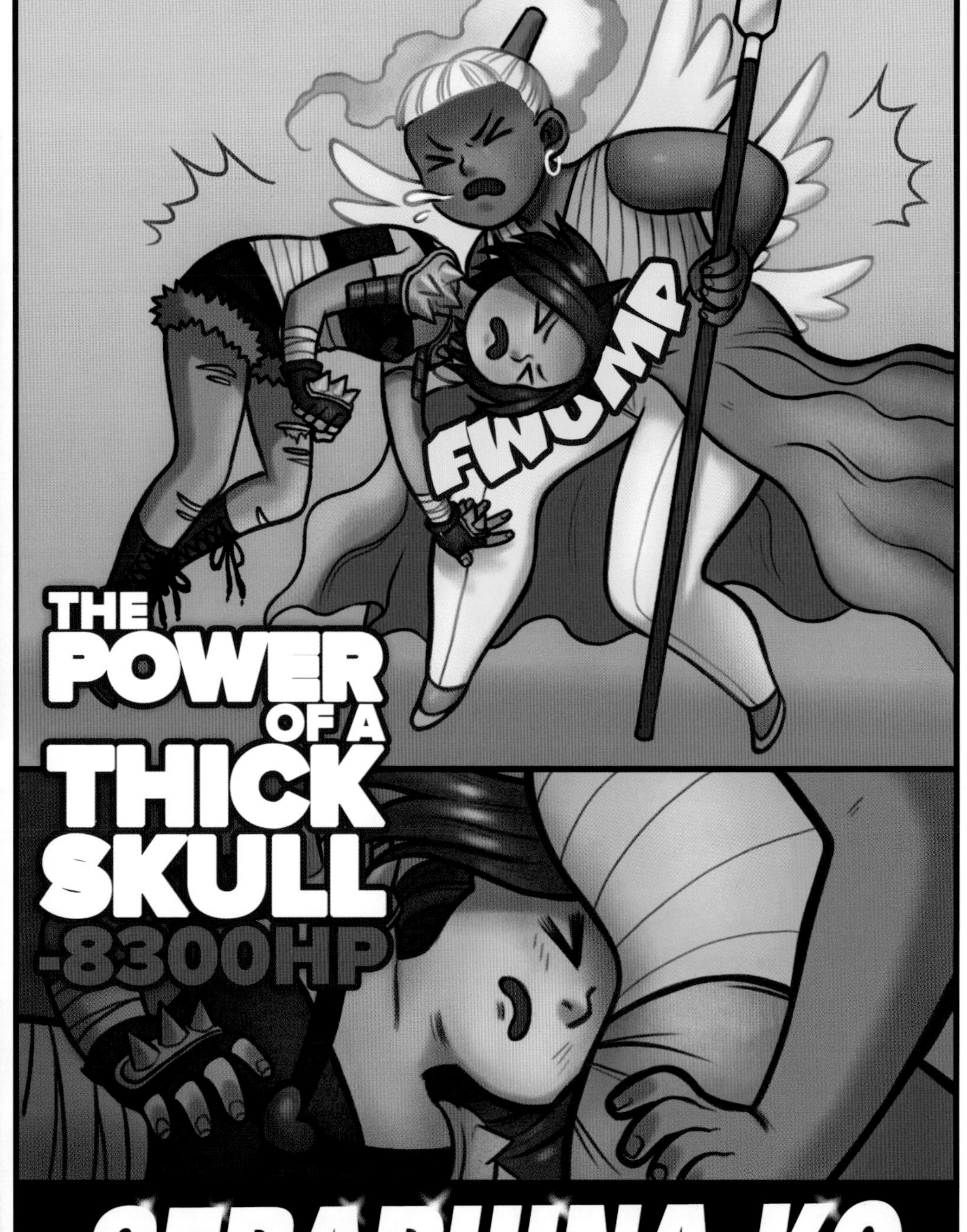

SERAPHINA KO

BATTLE COMPLETE

VICTORY: OLIVIA AND STELLA

REWARD FOR VICTORY

OLIVIA
+3 Levels (New Level: 25)

STELLA
+14 Levels (New Level: 18)

+1904 Crystal Points
New Item Yggdrasil Tincture x5
New Item Covalent Pin
New Item Angelic Feather
New Item Summoner's Crystal

STRONGEST SINGLE ATTACK:

Power of a Thick Skull
-8300HP

SPECTATORS' RATING:

THAT THING YOU DID BACK THERE...
WHAT WAS THAT?
I MEAN, I JUST TRIPPED ON MY--

NO, THE GAME WORLD... IT GLITCHED.
I'VE NEVER SEEN ANYTHING LIKE THAT BEFORE.

I--I DUNNO!
IT'S LIKE WHAT HAPPENED WHEN THE DOORWAY TO THE ARENA APPEARED!

IT'S POSSIBLE THAT YOUR *MASSIVE*, *ROCK-LIKE* SKULL GROWS LARGER WHEN YOU'RE ANGRY, PRESSING YOUR HEADSET'S CIRCUITRY TOGETHER IN NOVEL WAYS AND CREATING STRANGE GLITCHES IN THE GAME.

IT'S A WORKING THEORY.
TRUTHFULLY, I DON'T KNOW THE EXACT CAUSE.

WHATEVER THE CASE, *PENELOPE* SEEMED SURPRISED, WHICH I'VE ALSO NEVER SEEN BEFORE.

ANYWAY, WHEN YOU'RE DONE LEVELING, USE SOME *YGGDRASIL TINCTURE* TO HEAL YOURSELF.
LEVEL UP
STR
INT
VIT

TNX!

glug
glug

NOW THAT YOU'RE ALL HEALED UP, I THINK YOU SHOULD DO SOME TRAINING.
YOU DID ALL RIGHT OUT THERE, BUT THERE WERE A LOT OF CLOSE CALLS.
YOU CAN PRACTICE YOUR MOVES AGAINST AN AI OPPONENT IN HERE.
FOR NOW, I'LL KEEP IT ON EASY.

EASY, HUH?

shhiiifff
THUNK

FeeWWW
BOOM

YOU MIGHT WANT TO BUMP THE DIFFICULTY UP, DOC.
STELLA KIM?

PENELOPE HAS REQUESTED YOUR PRESENCE IN THE RING.
THIS WAY.

I'VE BEEN DEBATING HOW BEST TO PUNISH SOMEONE WHO NOT ONLY **HACKED** THEIR WAY INTO THE ARENA, BUT HAD THE AUDACITY TO ENTER THE RING!

AT FIRST I WAS GOING TO BAN YOUR HEADSET FROM CRYSTAL FIGHTERS ENTIRELY, BUT YOUR BATTLE AMUSED ME.
AND I'M RARELY AMUSED.

SO MY OFFER IS THIS:
EITHER EXIT IMMEDIATELY AND ACCEPT YOUR BAN, OR BATTLE MY FRIENDS HERE.
IF YOU BEAT THEM, I'LL GIVE YOU A KEY TO THE ARENA.

FINE.
I ACCEPT YOUR CHALLENGE.

PERFECT!
CHOOSE YOUR PARTNER AND WE'LL START THE BATTLE IMMEDIATELY!

COME ON, LET'S GET READY FOR THE FIGHT!
YEAH, ABOUT THAT...
YOU'RE ON YOUR OWN.

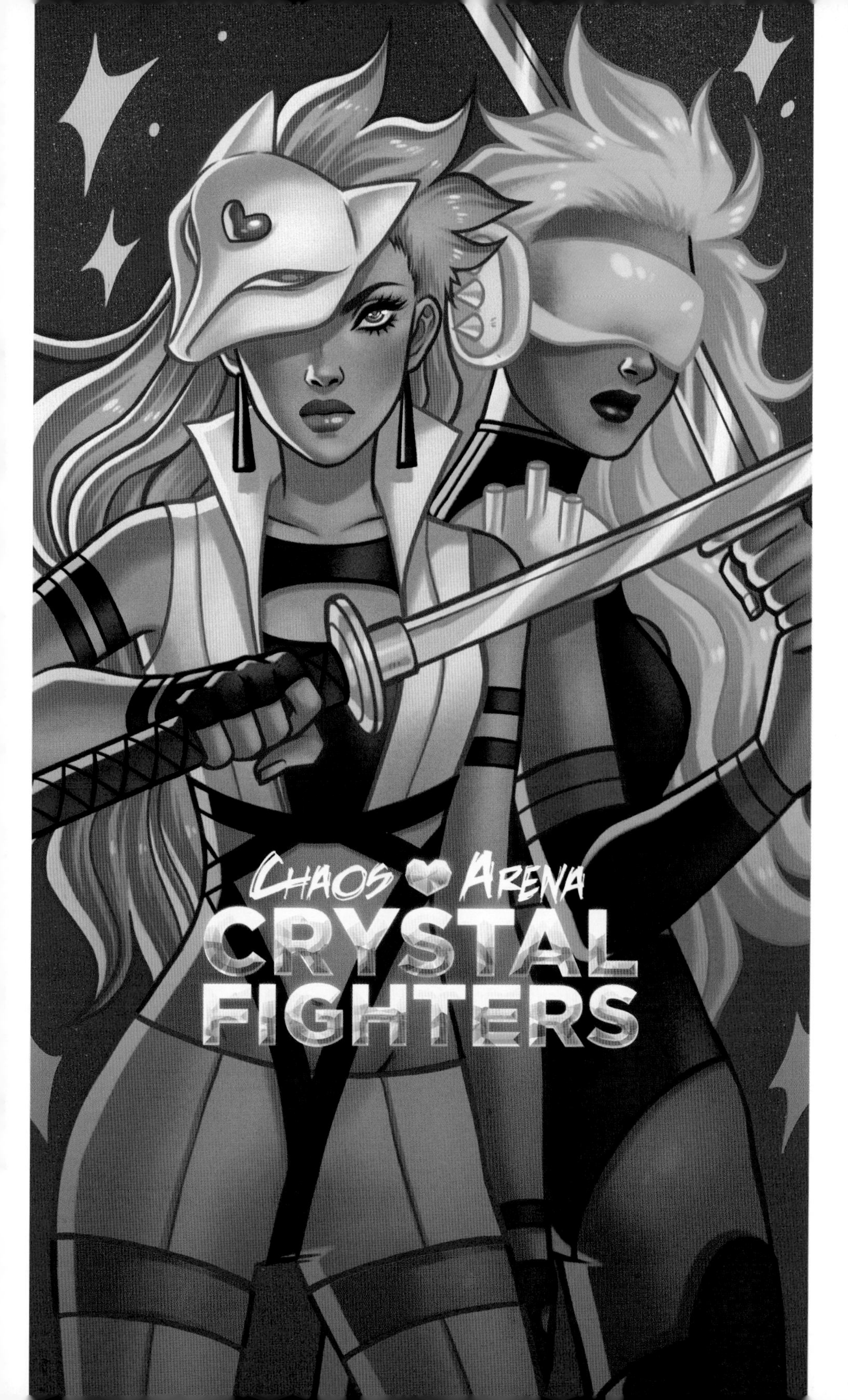
Chaos Arena
CRYSTAL FIGHTERS

AND BEFORE YOU GO, I'D LIKE TO REMIND YOU THAT YOUR FINAL DRAFTS ARE DUE NEXT TUESDAY.

RIIIINNGGG
I'M **SO** GLAD THE TEACHER DIDN'T CALL ON HER TODAY.
I CAN BARELY UNDERSTAND HER WITH THAT ACCENT.
hee hee hee

I CAN'T BELIEVE YOU HAVE THE NERVE TO--
OH, DON'T EVEN **START** ON THAT!!!

UGH.
GET A DIVORCE ALREADY!!
I AM SO SICK OF THEM AND THEIR CRUMMY RELATIONSHIP.

PENELOPE
PATEL
LEVEL 58
HP 8863
MP 4548
EXP 79541CP
LVL UP 101310CP

THIS BETTER BE ENTERTAINING.
TRAINING
WHAT DO YOU MEAN, YOU'RE NOT GOING TO FIGHT?
LOOK, I'M NOT PUTTING MY KEY ON THE LINE AGAINST THOSE TWO.

I'VE SEEN THEM FIGHT AND WE CAN'T BEAT THEM.
I'M SORRY, STELLA.
WE GAVE IT OUR BEST AND AT LEAST YOU TRIED...

NO.
I DIDN'T TRY-- I WON.

AND I'M GOING TO DO IT AGAIN, WITH OR WITHOUT YOU.
STR
INT
VIT
LUK
AGI
DEX

I THOUGHT YOU HAD MY BACK.

WAIT!
YOU DON'T UNDERSTAND WHAT YOU'RE UP AGAINST!

HOW LONG DO YOU THINK SHE'LL LAST, DIGIT?
TWO MINUTES? THREE?

1vs2 BATTLE:
STELLA
BIT
AND
DIGIT

LET THE CHAOS BEGIN!

SHEEWW

CUTE.
tink

ACK!!
THUNNPP

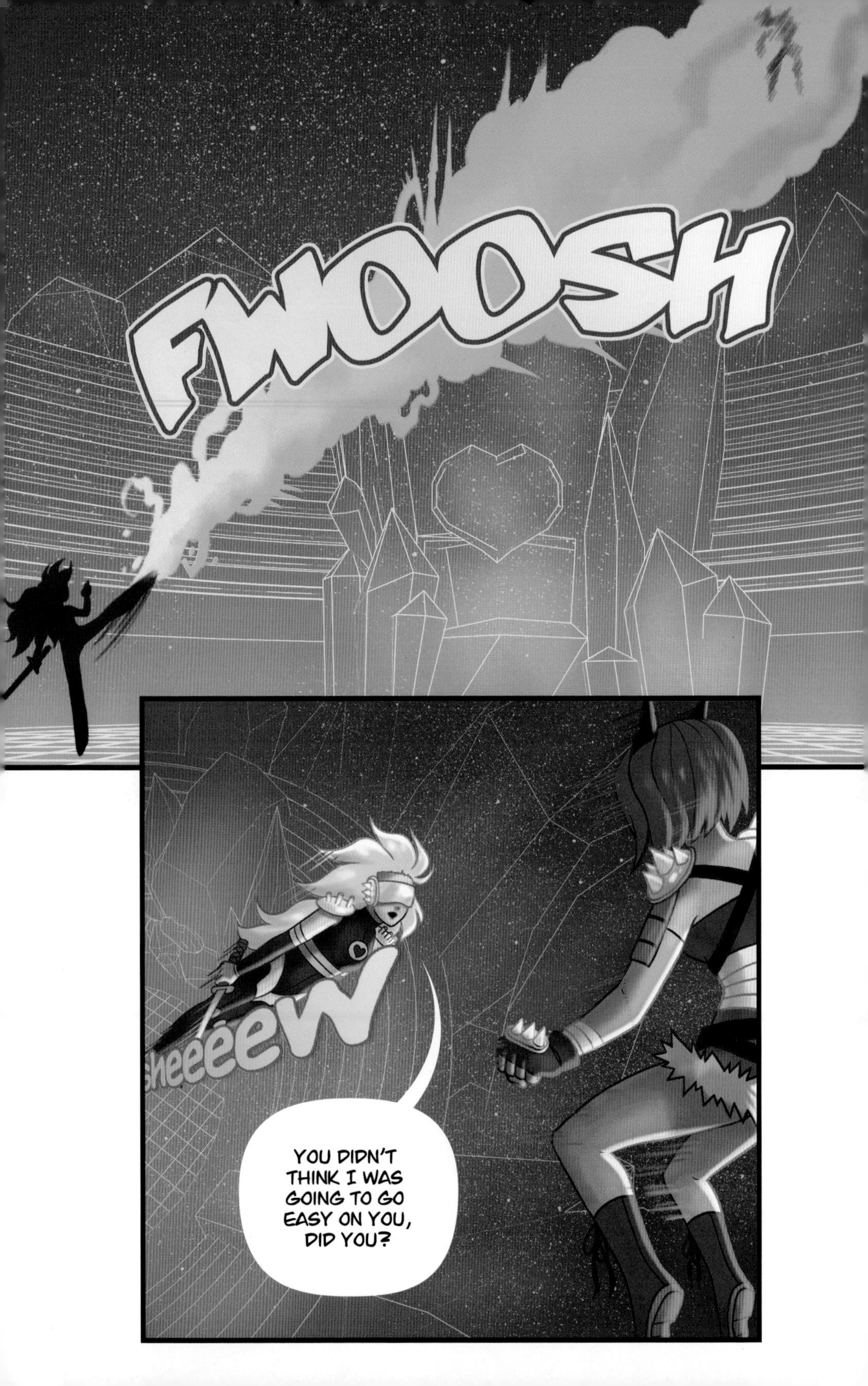
FWOOSH
sheeeew
YOU DIDN'T THINK I WAS GOING TO GO EASY ON YOU, DID YOU?

POW!
KRACK

AUUGGHH.
KRUNK!
JACKPOT.

THIS ENDS NOW.

STELLA KO
AHHH!
SHECK

ARE YOU SERIOUS?
THAT WAS IT?

UGH, THIS IS EXACTLY WHAT I *TRIED* TO WARN HER ABOUT.
I CAN'T LET THIS INTERRUPT THE COUNCIL'S PLAN FOR HER...

REALLY, DIGIT?
YOU DIDN'T LET ME GET A SINGLE HIT IN!
SORRY.

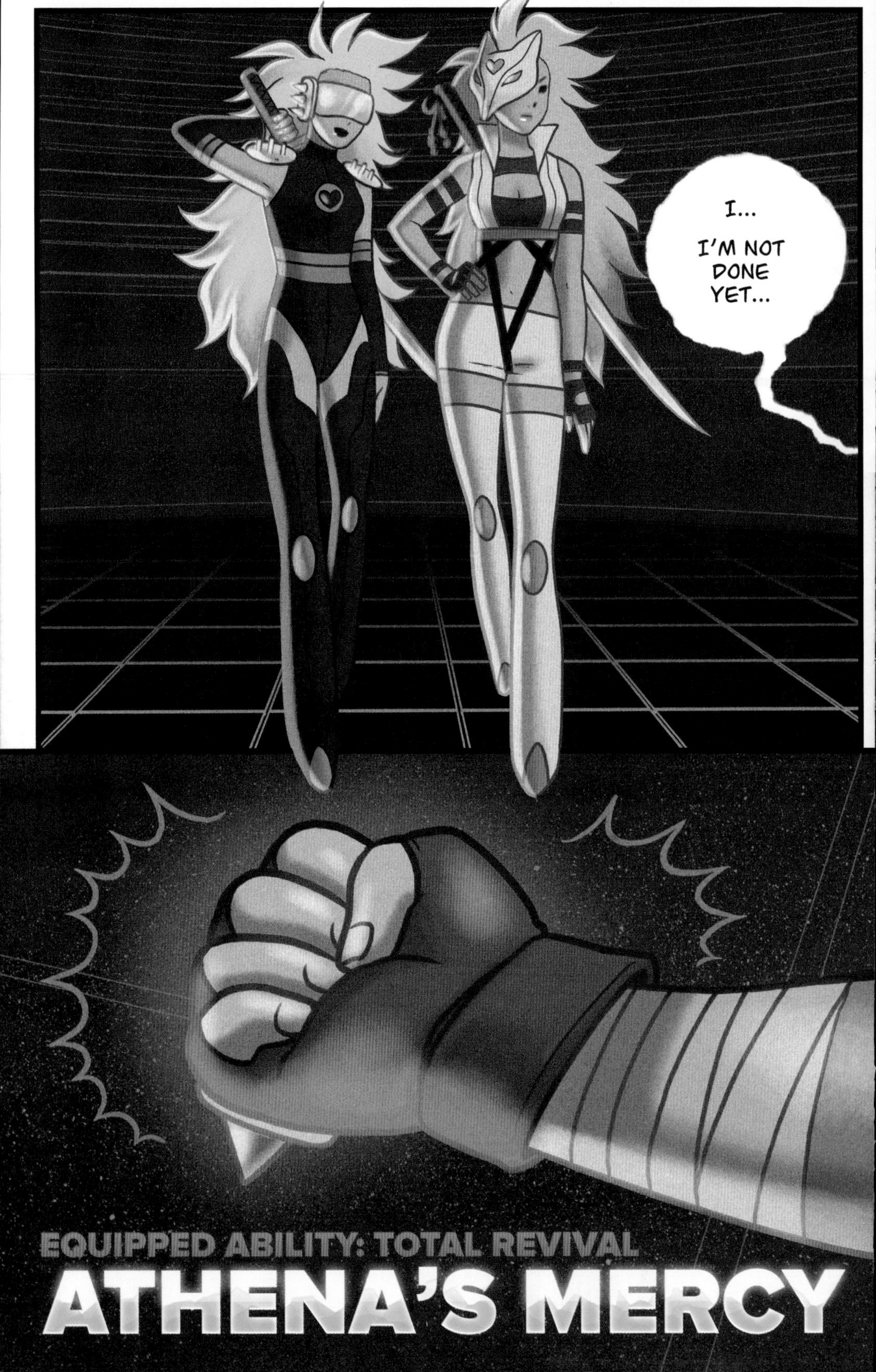

I...

I'M NOT DONE YET...

EQUIPPED ABILITY: TOTAL REVIVAL

ATHENA'S MERCY

EVEN IF NOBODY BELIEVES IN ME, I'VE TRAINED HARD...
I DESERVE TO BE HERE...
AND I'M NOT GOING TO LET YOU TAKE THAT FROM ME!
BITE OF THE WEEPING DRAGONS

YYAAHH

DUDE, YOUR HAIR...
HAHAHAHAHAHAHAHAHAHAHAHAHAHAHA
HAHA
HA
HAHA

SPECIAL ATTACK

TRANSDIMENSIONAL SHIFT!

WHAT THE...

-16000
...FRICK!!
STELLA KO

HAHAHAHA
HAHAHAHA
HAHAHAHA
HAHAHAHA
HAHA

GUESS SHE WASN'T CUT OUT FOR THIS AFTER ALL.

ARGH
HAHAHAHAHAHAHA

UGGHH...
I KNEW IT.

I SPENT THE REST OF THE WEEKEND SULKING.
IT'S PRETTY HARD TO STAY FOCUSED WHEN GETTING HUMILIATED IN FRONT OF HUNDREDS OF PEOPLE IS STILL FRESH IN YOUR MIND.

THE WORST PART IS I CAN'T GO ANYWHERE WITHOUT HEARING SOMEONE TALK ABOUT THE GAME.
I'M SO EXCITED FOR THE *CRYSTAL FIGHTERS* EXPANSION PACK THEY'RE RELEASING NEXT WEEK!!

I KEEP REPLAYING IT IN MY MIND.
COULD I HAVE DONE SOMETHING DIFFERENTLY?
I MEAN, MAYBE IF OLIVIA...
STELLA...?

I'M OLIVIA--
FROM THE ARENA.
!
LOOK, WE
NEED TO TALK.

CHAOS ARENA
CRYSTAL FIGHTERS

I--I STILL CAN'T BELIEVE YOU GO TO THE SAME SCHOOL AS ME!
THERE'S ACTUALLY A LOT OF CHAOS ARENA MEMBERS HERE...
BUT THAT'S A STORY FOR ANOTHER TIME.
ANYWAY, I JUST WANT TO APOLOGIZE FOR WHAT HAPPENED--

OH.
RIGHT.
THAT.
IT'S NOT THAT I DIDN'T WANT TO HELP, BUT YOU WENT IN THERE WITH NO PLAN AND SIGNED US BOTH UP TO BE SLAUGHTERED!
HMPF.
THE ARENA IS REALLY IMPORTANT TO ME. I COULDN'T PUT MY KEY ON THE LINE FOR A BATTLE I KNEW WE COULDN'T WIN.
BUT I THINK I KNOW HOW TO MAKE IT UP TO YOU.

WHAT DO YOU MEAN?
JUST MEET ME IN THE GAME AT FOUR O'CLOCK.
I HAVE SOMETHING TO SHOW YOU THAT--WELL, IF IT WORKS--MIGHT CHANGE EVERYTHING.
I'LL SEE IF I CAN FIT IT IN.
I LEAD A BUSY LIFE AND IT'S DIFFICULT TO FIND TIME FOR THIS KIND OF STUFF.

I LIED.
I HAVE ABSOLUTELY NOTHING GOING ON.
I'M STILL UPSET THAT OLIVIA ABANDONED ME WHEN I NEEDED HER...
BUT I HAVE TO FIND OUT WHAT SHE WAS TALKING ABOUT AT SCHOOL.

WELCOME TO CRYSTAL FIGHTERS! ENJOY YOUR GAME!
OH YAY, *THIS* AGAIN.
IT LOOKS LIKE YOU WERE ABLE TO FIT ME INTO YOUR BUSY SCHEDULE, HUH?
WEREN'T YOU SUPPOSED TO BE APOLOGIZING OR SOMETHING LIKE THAT?
SOMETHING LIKE THAT.

STAY THERE!

I HOPE *THEY* WERE RIGHT ABOUT THIS...

FOOM
PEW
POOF
PSHEW
CRYSTAL SUMMON
COUSIN JESSICA:
THE ENDLESSLY
UNWAVERING AND UNREQUITED

JESSICA
ESSICA
ICAAAA

STEELLLLS!
SHOOOM
NOW WE
CAN BE
LIKE, BFFS x50...

THIS IS WHAT YOU WANTED TO SHOW ME?!
PSSH
BESHUUM
PYEW
AHHHHHG!
POOM

HAH!
I KNEW IT!

WAIT--WHAT?! HOW DID WE--
DON'T YOU GET IT, STELLA? IT WASN'T AN ACCIDENT THAT YOU ENDED UP IN THE ARENA.
THAT ABILITY OF YOURS TO GLITCH THE GAME-- YOU HAVE SOME KIND OF SPECIAL POWER.

IF YOU GET ANGRY ENOUGH, IT TRIGGERS A CHANGE IN THE WAY THE GAME WORKS.
I MEAN, THINK ABOUT IT!
THERE'S NO WAY YOU SHOULD HAVE BEEN ABLE TO KO SERAPHINA WITH THE LEVEL YOU WERE AT, EVEN IF YOU DO HAVE A HEAD LIKE A WRECKING BALL.

HEAD LIKE A--SO ARE WE JUST ACCEPTING THAT AS FACT NOW?

IF YOU CAN HARNESS YOUR POWER, I REALLY THINK YOU STAND A CHANCE OF WINNING AGAINST--

I CAN'T BELIEVE YOU BROUGHT ME HERE FOR *THIS!* AS IF I WANT TO SUBJECT MYSELF TO THAT KIND OF HUMILATION AGAIN!
THANKS, BUT I'M DONE WITH THIS GAME.

OH, COME ON! YOU AND I BOTH KNOW THAT'S NOT TRUE!
THE ARENA IS THE ONLY PLACE IN THIS WHOLE GAME WHERE WE GET TO BE WHO WE REALLY ARE!

...
YOU CAN DO THIS, STELLA.
WE CAN DO THIS TOGETHER.
IF YOU REALLY THINK YOU CAN HELP ME CONTROL THIS...

...I'M IN.

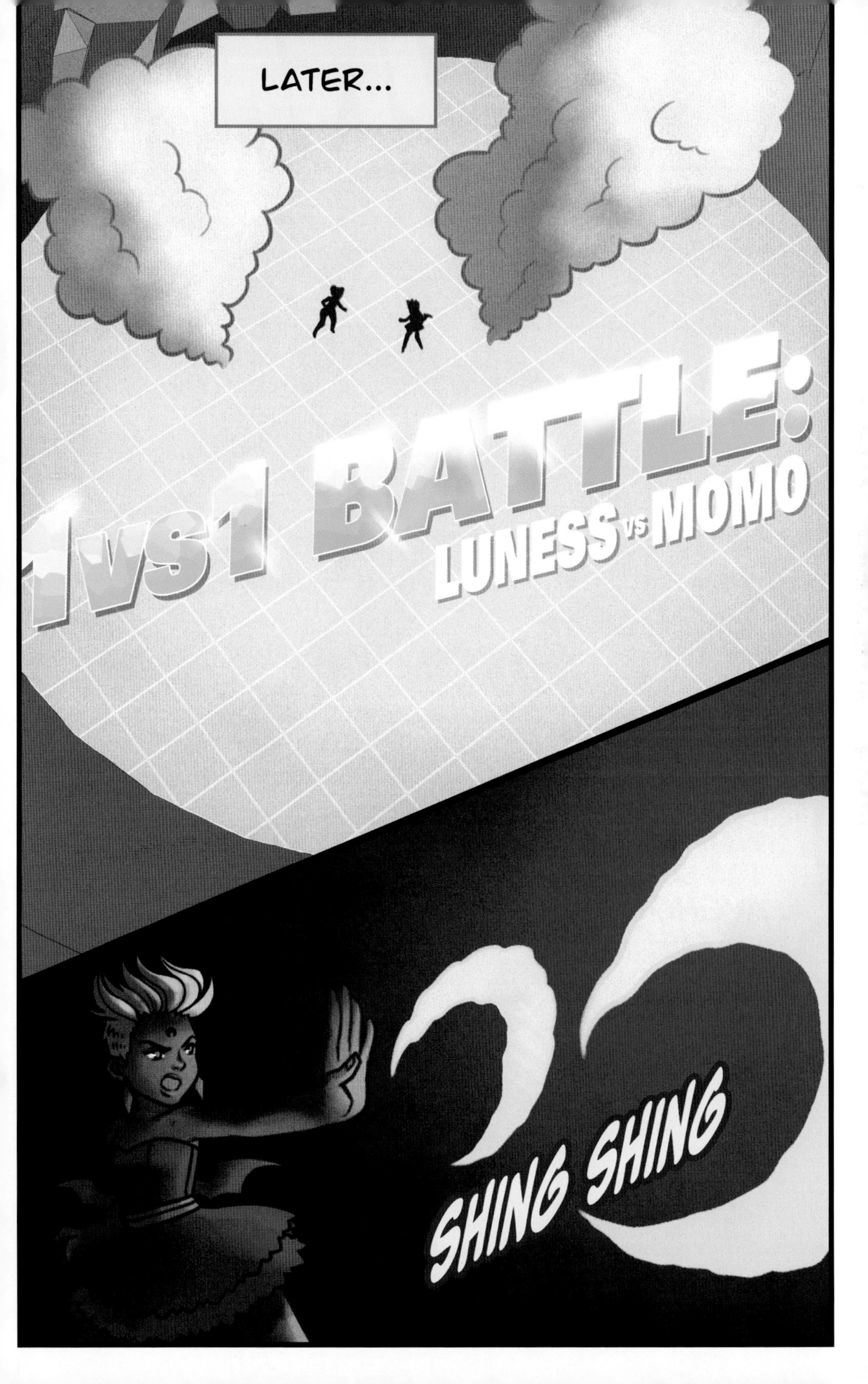
LATER...
1VS1 BATTLE:
LUNESS VS MOMO
SHING SHING

ZRRINNGG
I'VE BEEN WAITING FAR TOO LONG TO AVENGE MY SIS--

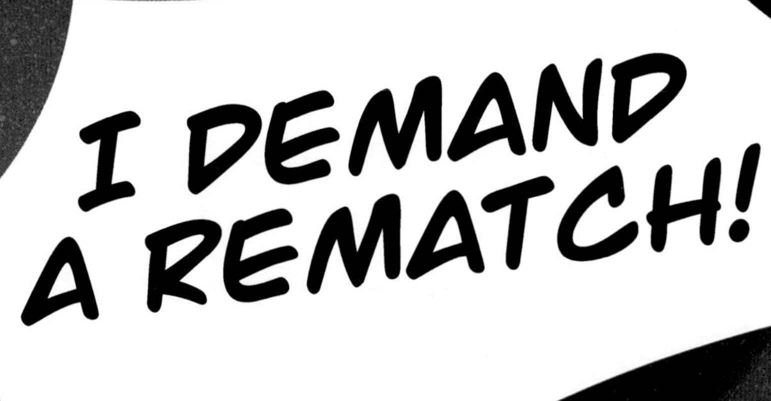

I DEMAND A REMATCH!

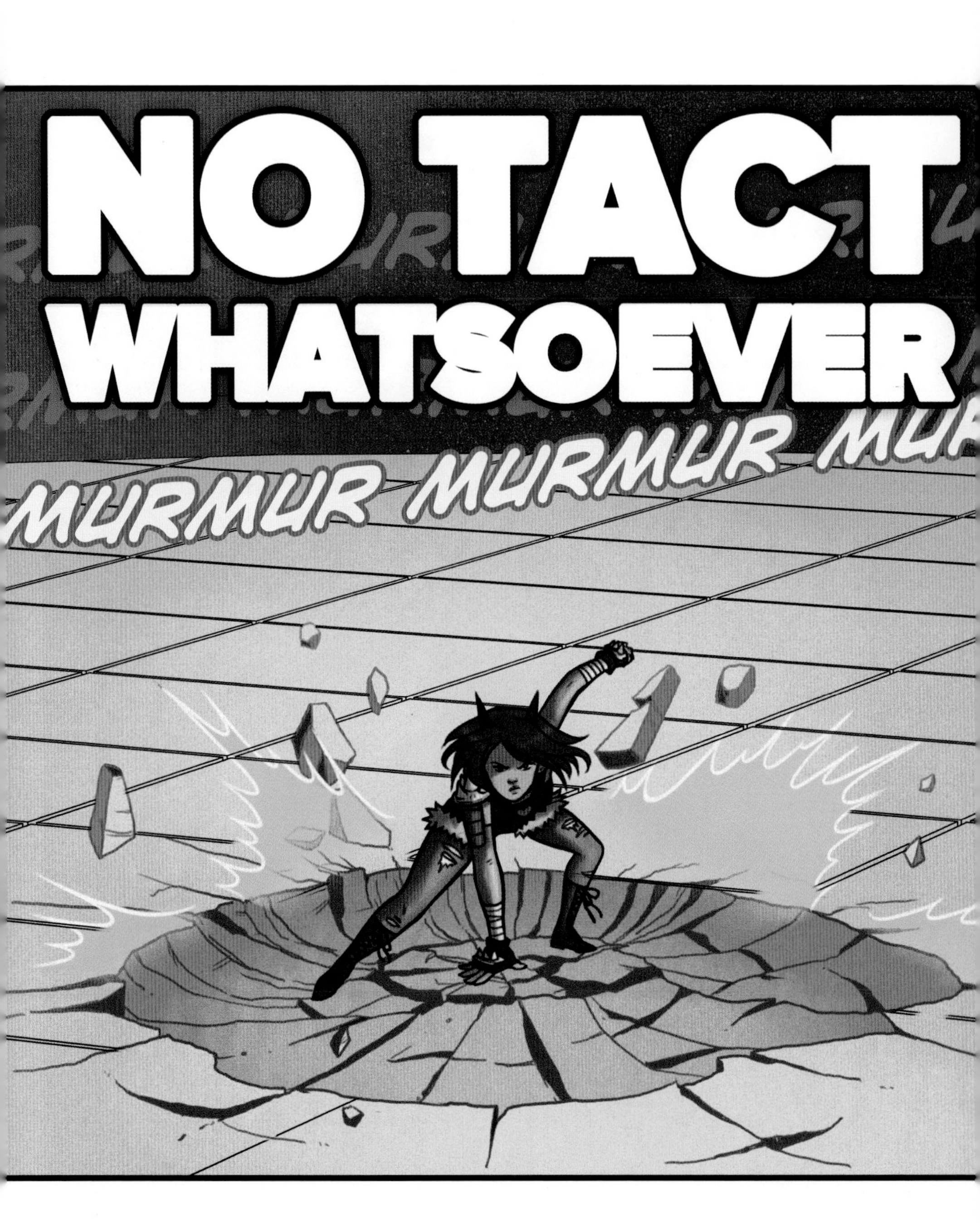
NO TACT WHATSOEVER
MURMUR MURMUR MURMUR

YOU'VE GOT TO BE KIDDING ME...
WHAT THE?! YOU CAN'T JUST INTERRUPT OUR FIGHT LIKE THAT!!
SILENCE!
HOW DID YOU GET BACK IN HERE?!

WE'LL GET TO THAT AFTER I TAKE CARE OF YOUR LACKEYS!
NO WAY!
THIS LITTLE PUNK ACTUALLY CAME BACK ASKING FOR MORE!

JUST DISPOSE OF HER QUICKLY.
THE NOVETLY HAS WORN OFF.

SHISH
SHO

YOU BACK FOR ANOTHER HAIRCUT?
HOLD UP.
YOU GOT TO HAVE ALL THE FUN LAST TIME.

DIGIT FINISHED YOU OFF TOO QUICKLY BEFORE.
SEE, IF THAT HAD BEEN *ME* YOU WERE FIGHTING, YOU WOULDN'T BE BACK HERE ASKING FOR MORE...
NOT THAT I'M COMPLAINING.
I GET TO BE THE ONE THAT KNOCKS YOU OUT IN FRONT OF THE AUDIENCE FOR A *THIRD TIME*.

I CAN DO THIS...
grrrrr

JUST THINK...
ANGRY THOUGHTS...

...YOUR ROCK-LIKE HEAD...
YOU'RE ALMOST A WOMAN, STELLA!
START ACTING LIKE ONE!
GUESS SHE WASN'T CUT OUT FOR THIS AFTER ALL!

NOW WE CAN BE, LIKE, BFFS x50!!
...LIKE, BFFS x50...
B F F S
YAAAAHHH

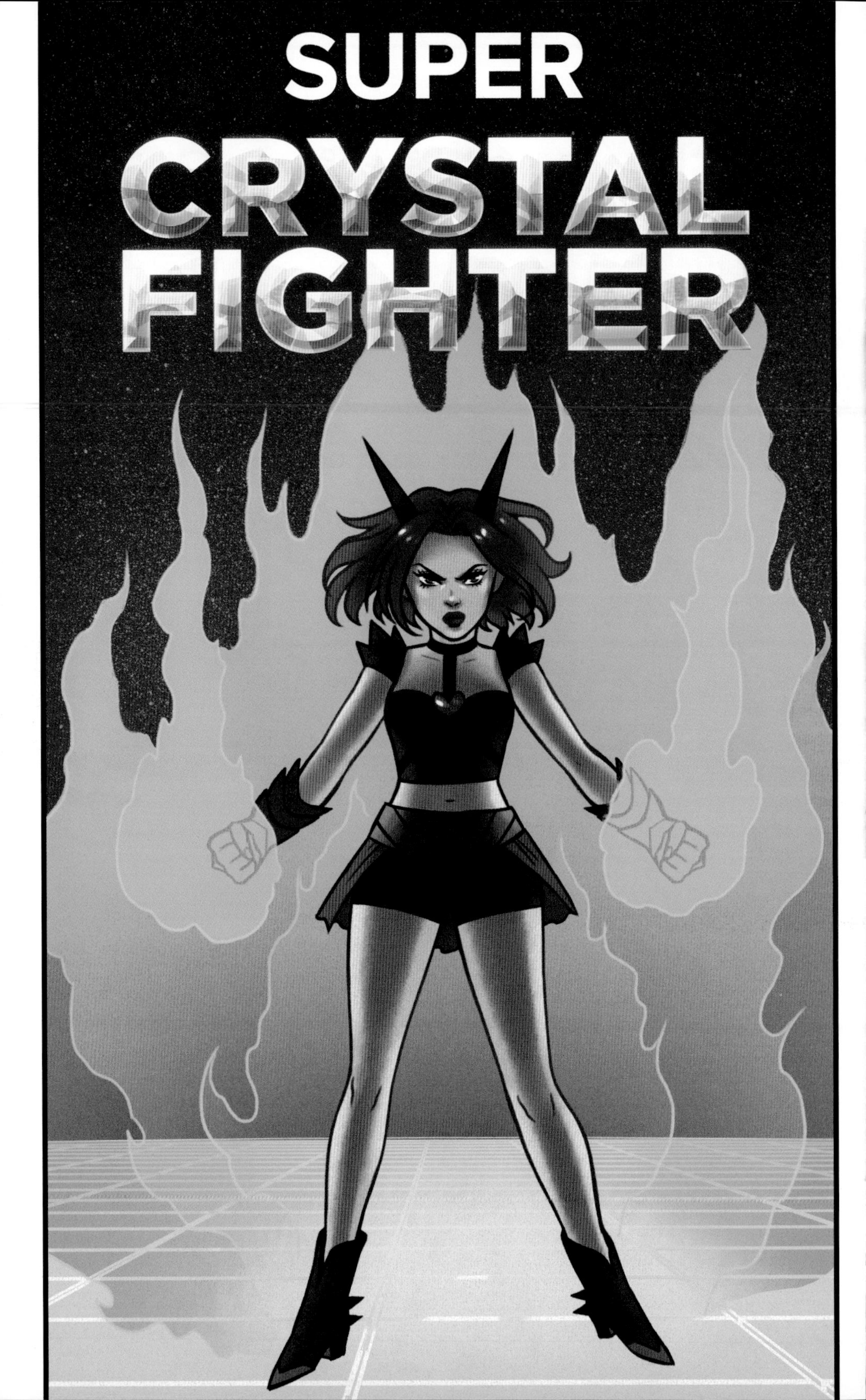
SUPER
CRYSTAL
FIGHTER

HEY, BIT!

BLAM
IS THIS AS MUCH FUN AS YOU THOUGHT IT WOULD BE?
SIIZZZZ

N-NO WAY...
KLOMP
KLOMP

ZZHHOOOOM
SHA-KOOM
BIT KO

THWUMP
KKKKRKK
KRUNK
DIGIT KO

SO WHERE'S THAT KEY, PENELOPE?
I TOOK THEM OUT--A DEAL'S A DEAL!

FWOOOSH

SORRY, THAT WAS THE DEAL LAST TIME.
IF YOU STILL WANT THAT KEY, YOU HAVE TO GO THROUGH ME.

Chaos Arena
CRYSTAL FIGHTERS

A DEAL'S A DEAL!
HAND OVER THE KEY YOU PROMISED ME!

IF YOU WANT THE KEY...
BOSS FIGHT:
PENELOPE vs STELLA

...COME TAKE IT!

AHHHHHH

THIS IS MY ARENA!
I GAVE YOU A CHANCE TO PROVE YOURSELF...
SHNG
EEP!

AND YOU FAILED!
FWUSH

AAHHHHH
SPECIAL ATTACK
THE INEVITABLE END

KUH-DOOO
ACK!
THUUUM

SHOOOSH
AAHH!

EGHH...
I HAVE TO ADMIT, THIS WHOLE SUPER CRYSTAL FIGHTER THING IS AN IMPRESSIVE PARTY TRICK.
BUT IT'S GOING TO TAKE A LOT MORE THAN A COSTUME CHANGE TO BEAT ME.

OH, THE OUTFIT IS JUST FOR MY FAN CLUB!
♥ YOU STELLA!
SHAAAAHHHH
FOR YOU--
WELL, I'VE GOT SOMETHING SPECIAL FOR YOU.
SPECIAL ATTACK
HOMING KNUCKLES

DODGE THIS!
PESHOOO
!

BOOM
FAAASHH
THNNGGG

HOLY CRAP, IS THIS REAL?!
DID SHE ACTUALLY MANAGE TO TAKE DOWN PENELOPE?
I CAN'T BELIEVE IT!
PRETTY RAD!
SHE'S NOT OUT OF THE WOODS YET...

AWW LOOK, SHE LEFT ME A SOUVENIER!

MAYBE I CAN USE IT TO CHISEL THAT STUPID HEART OFF THE THRONE NOW THAT I'LL BE--

KRAKKK
YAAH!
SHOOO
THWAK

STOP!
THIS-- THIS IS NOT OKAY.
DO YOU HAVE ANY IDEA HOW HARD IT IS TO FIND A HAT THAT FITS MY HEAD **NORMALLY**?

THUNK
HERE, I'LL EVEN IT BACK OUT FOR YOU.

Sheeeww

IT DIDN'T HAVE TO BE THIS WAY!
YOU COULD'VE JUST GIVEN ME THE KEY LIKE YOU PROMISED AND SPARED YOURSELF THE EMBARRASSMENT OF LOSING IN FRONT OF THE CROWD!

YOU ARROGANT LITTLE--
zzhmm
veewssh

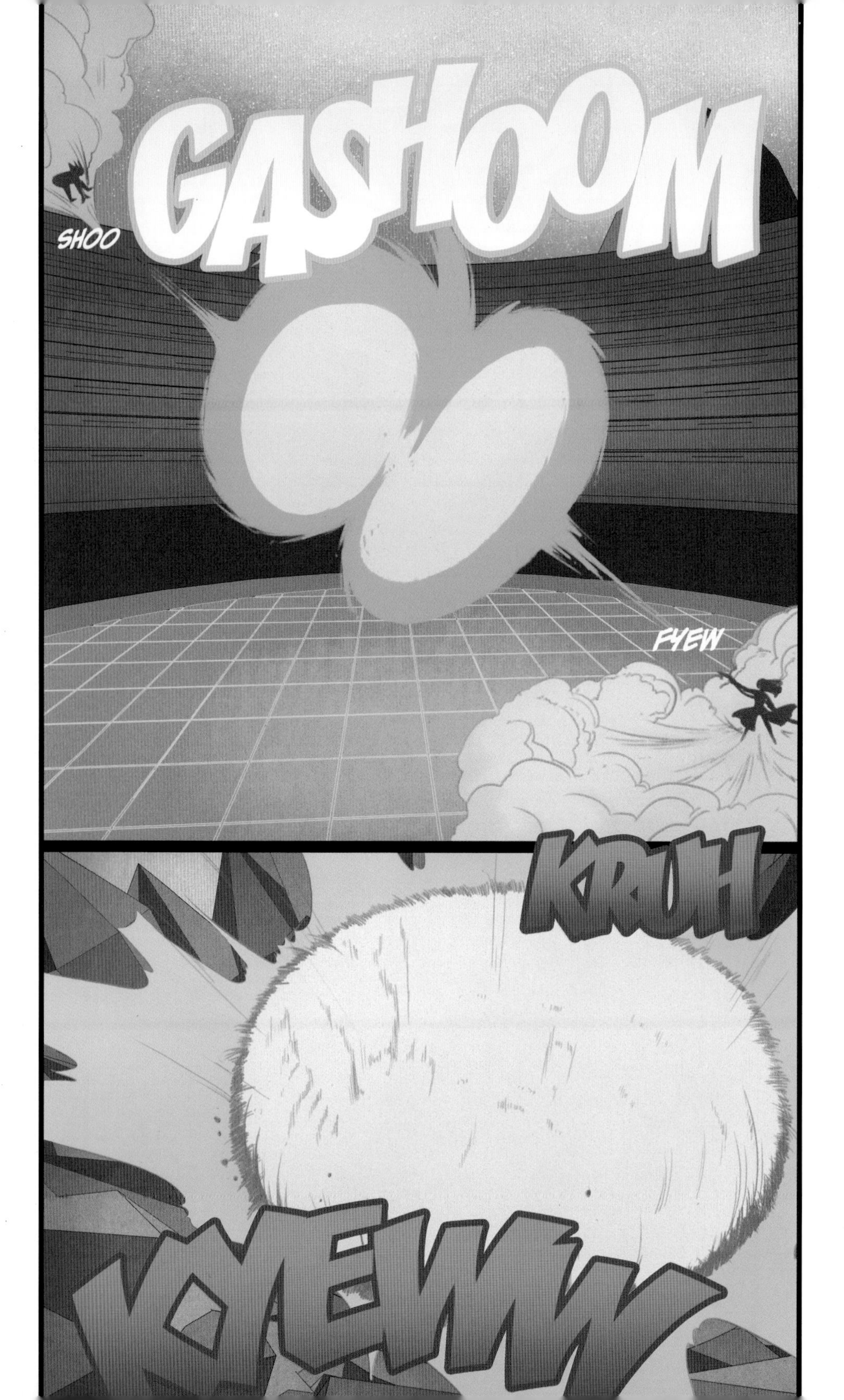
GASHOOM
SHOO
FYEW
KRUH
KYEWW

ASP
WHEEEEZ
HACK
COUGH
FSSSHHHHH
I CAN'T SEE ANYTHING.
NO WAY... I THINK THEY'RE STILL STANDING.

HUFF
HUFF

THAT ALL YOU GOT?

I'M JUST GETTING STARTED.

YAAAAHH
STOP!

THIS IS OVER!
HUH? WAIT A SECOND... I THOUGHT YOU LOOKED FAMILIAR!
YOU'RE HERE ON BEHALF OF THE COUNCIL, AREN'T YOU?

THAT'S RIGHT.
STELLA, THE CHAOS CLUB HAS BEEN MONITORING YOU SINCE THAT GLITCH LED YOU INTO THE ARENA.
WUHHH?

THEY SAW YOUR UNIQUE POWER, BUT WEREN'T CONVINCED YOU COULD LEARN TO CONTROL IT.
THEY SENT ME TO SEE IF YOU COULD LEARN TO HARNESS YOUR ABILITIES.

THEY TOLD ME I WAS IN CHARGE OF DEALING WITH HER!
I'M NOT GOING TO TOLERATE ONE OF THEIR *MOLES* COMING IN HERE AND INTERRUPTING A FIGHT!

IF YOU HAVE A PROBLEM, TAKE IT UP WITH THEM.

WAIT, SO THIS WAS ALL SOME KIND OF TEST?
THINK OF IT AS...AN OPPORTUNITY.

THEY'D LIKE TO INVITE YOU TO PARTICIPATE IN *THE TOURNAMENT OF MASTERS.*
THE STRONGEST FIGHTERS FROM ALL TEN GLOBAL SERVERS ARE GATHERING IN THE *SHADOW CITY* OF **CERES** TO COMPETE IN A SERIES OF BATTLES.
THE WINNERS WILL BECOME THE NEW REGIONAL RINGMASTERS, MEANING--

WHAT?!
THEY CAN'T BE SERIOUS ABOUT INVITING HER TO THE TOURNAMENT!
SHE IS NOWHERE NEAR THE LEVEL THE REST OF US ARE!
IF THEY TRULY THINK--
LADY PENELOPE! THE COUNCIL HAS REQUESTED YOUR PRESENCE!

FINE. I'LL SPEAK TO THEM DIRECTLY.
BUT NEXT TIME, THERE WON'T BE ANY INTERRUPTIONS TO SAVE HER.

GRR...
DON'T LET HER GET TO YOU.

MAYBE THIS WILL MAKE YOU FEEL BETTER...
A GIFT FROM THE CHAOS CLUB.

A GIFT? COULD THIS BE WHAT I--
NO WAY!!

NEW ITEM ACQUIRED

DECRYPTION KEY

Grants entrance to Chaos Club servers.

MY VERY OWN KEY!
HOLD UP, YOUR WORK'S NOT OVER.

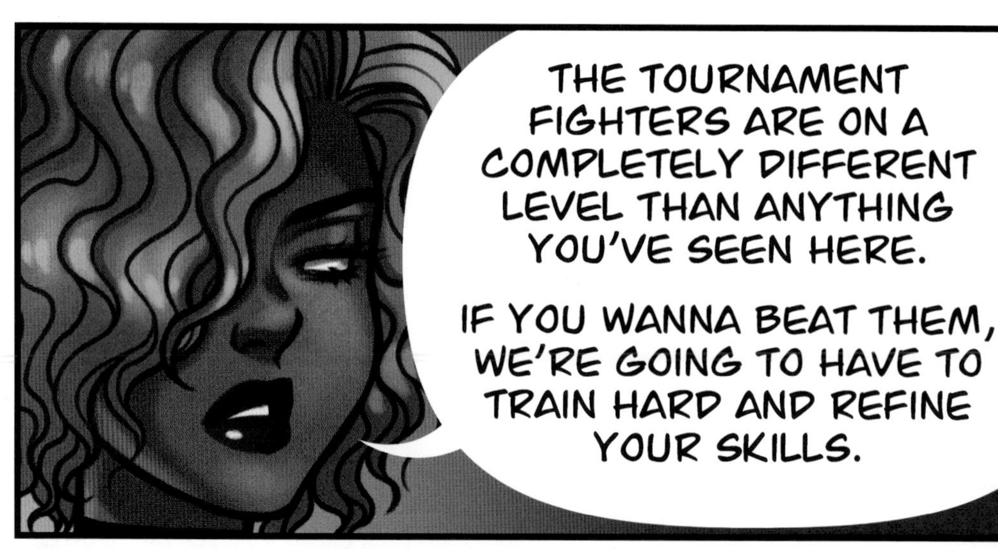
THE TOURNAMENT FIGHTERS ARE ON A COMPLETELY DIFFERENT LEVEL THAN ANYTHING YOU'VE SEEN HERE.
IF YOU WANNA BEAT THEM, WE'RE GOING TO HAVE TO TRAIN HARD AND REFINE YOUR SKILLS.

WE? PSSHT.
YOU KEPT ME IN THE DARK ABOUT *EVERYTHING* UNTIL JUST NOW!
YOU'RE A PART OF SOME SECRET CLUB AND YOU DIDN'T SAY ANYTHING?
WHY SHOULD I TRUST YOU?

IT'S A LITTLE MORE COMPLICATED THAN THAT.
EITHER WAY, WE GOT THIS FAR TOGETHER. YOU'RE REALLY GOING TO THROW THAT ALL AWAY OVER ONE SECRET?
LOOK, I'LL TELL YOU ANYTHING YOU WANT TO KNOW ON THE WAY TO THE TOURNAMENT.

HMPF. ALL RIGHT.
BUT FROM HERE ON OUT, NO MORE SECRETS, OKAY?
UNDERSTOOD.
NOW BEFORE WE HEAD TO THE TOURNAMENT, I'VE GOT A FEW THINGS TO TAKE CARE OF OFFLINE.

HEAD TO THE TRAINING ROOM AND START PREPPING.
I'LL MEET YOU THERE IN FIFTEEN MINUTES.

GOT IT. LET'S DO THIS.
I GUESS DAD WAS RIGHT-- CRYSTAL FIGHTERS IS PRETTY FUN...
ONCE YOU, Y'KNOW, STRIP OUT ALL OF THE RULES AND ALLOW THE PLAYERS TO VICIOUSLY BEAT EACH OTHER.

BUT IT'S NICE TO FINALLY HAVE A PLACE THAT ACCEPTS ME FOR WHO I AM. A VIRTUAL WORLD FILLED WITH REAL FRIENDS.

EVERYTHING WENT AS YOU SAID IT WOULD.

WE'LL START PHASE TWO ONCE SHE ARRIVES AT THE TOURNAMENT.
SHE HAS NO IDEA WHAT'S COMING.
EXCELLENT.
END

MORE TITLES YOU MIGHT ENJOY

AXE COP

Malachai Nicolle, Ethan Nicolle

Bad guys, beware! Evil aliens, run for your lives! Axe Cop is here, and he's going to chop your head off! We live in a strange world, and our strange problems call for strange heroes. That's why Axe Cop is holding tryouts to build the greatest team of heroes ever assembled.

Volume 1 ISBN 978-1-59582-681-7 $14.99
Volume 2 ISBN 978-1-59582-825-5 $14.99
Volume 3 ISBN 978-1-59582-911-5 $14.99
Volume 4 ISBN 978-1-61655-057-8 $12.99
Volume 5 ISBN 978-1-61655-245-9 $14.99
Volume 6 ISBN 978-1-61655-424-8 $12.99

THE ADVENTURES OF DR. MCNINJA OMNIBUS

Christopher Hastings

He's a doctor! He's a ninja! And now, his earliest exploits are collected in one mighty omnibus volume! Featuring stories from the very beginnings of the Dr. McNinja web comic, this book offers a hefty dose of science, action, and outrageous comedy.

$24.99 | ISBN 978-1-61655-112-4

BREATH OF BONES: A TALE OF THE GOLEM

Steve Niles, Matt Santoro, Dave Wachter

A British plane crashes in a Jewish village, sparking a Nazi invasion. Using clay and mud from the river, the villagers bring to life a giant monster to battle for their freedom and future.

$14.99 | ISBN 978-1-61655-344-9

REBELS

Brian Wood, Andrea Mutti, Matthew Woodson, Ariela Kristantina, Tristan Jones

This is 1775. With the War for Independence playing out across the colonies, Seth and Mercy Abbott find their new marriage tested at every turn as the demands of the frontlines and the home front collide.

Volume 1: A Well-Regulated Militia
$24.99 | ISBN 978-1-61655-908-3

HOW TO TALK TO GIRLS AT PARTIES

Neil Gaiman, Gabriel Bá, Fábio Moon

Two teenage boys are in for a tremendous shock when they crash a party where the girls are far more than they appear!

$17.99 | ISBN 978-1-61655-955-7

NANJING: THE BURNING CITY

Ethan Young

After the bombs fell, the Imperial Japanese Army seized the Chinese capital of Nanjing. Two abandoned Chinese soldiers try to escape the city and what they'll encounter will haunt them. But in the face of horror, they'll learn that resistance and bravery cannot be destroyed.

$24.99 | ISBN 978-1-61655-752-2

THE BATTLES OF BRIDGET LEE: INVASION OF FARFALL

Ethan Young

There is no longer a generation that remembers a time before the Marauders invaded Earth. Bridget Lee, an ex–combat medic now residing at the outpost Farfall, may be the world's last hope. But Bridget will need to overcome her own fears before she can save her people.

$10.99 | ISBN 978-1-50670-012-0

MORE TITLES YOU MIGHT ENJOY

HARROW COUNTY

Cullen Bunn, Tyler Crook

Emmy always knew that the woods surrounding her home crawled with ghosts and monsters. But on the eve of her eighteenth birthday, she learns that she is connected to these creatures—and to the land itself—in a way she never imagined.

$14.99 each

Volume 1: Countless Haints	ISBN 978-1-61655-780-5
Volume 2: Twice Told	ISBN 978-1-61655-900-7
Volume 3: Snake Doctor	ISBN 978-1-50670-071-7
Volume 4: Family Tree	ISBN 978-1-50670-141-7
Volume 5: Abandoned	ISBN 978-1-50670-190-5

SPACE-MULLET!

Daniel Warren Johnson

Ex–Space Marine Jonah and his copilot Alphius rove the galaxy, trying to get by. Drawn into one crazy adventure after another, they forge a crew of misfits into a family and face the darkest parts of the universe together.

$17.99 | ISBN 978-1-61655-912-0

EI8HT

Mike Johnson, Rafael Albuquerque

Welcome to the Meld, an inhospitable dimension in time where a chrononaut finds himself trapped. With no memory or feedback from the team of scientists that sent him, he can't count on anything but his heart and a stranger's voice to guide him to his destiny.

$17.99 | ISBN 978-1-61655-637-2

MUHAMMAD ALI

Sybille Titeux, Amazing Ameziane

Celebrating the life of the glorious athlete who metamorphosed from Cassius Clay to become a three-time heavyweight boxing legend, activist, and provocateur, Muhammad Ali is not only a titan in the world of sports but in the world itself, he dared to be different and to challenge and defy. Witness what made Ali different, what made him cool, what made him the Greatest.

$19.99 | ISBN 978-1-50670-318-3

THE FIFTH BEATLE: THE BRIAN EPSTEIN STORY

Vivek J. Tiwary, Andrew C. Robinson, Kyle Baker

The untold true story of Brian Epstein, the visionary manager who discovered and guided the Beatles to unprecedented international stardom. *The Fifth Beatle* is an uplifting, tragic, and ultimately inspirational human story about the struggle to overcome the odds..

$19.99 | ISBN 978-1-61655-256-5

Expanded Edition $14.99 | ISBN 978-1-61655-835-2

THE USAGI YOJIMBO SAGA

Stan Sakai

When a peace came upon Japan and samurai warriors found themselves suddenly unemployed and many of these ronin turned to banditry, found work, or traveled the musha shugyo to hone their spiritual and martial skills. Whether they took the honest road or the crooked path, the ronin were less than welcome. Such is the tale of Usagi Yojimbo.

$24.99 each

Volume 1	ISBN 978-1-61655-609-9
Volume 2	ISBN 978-1-61655-610-5
Volume 3	ISBN 978-1-61655-611-2
Volume 4	ISBN 978-1-61655-612-9
Volume 5	ISBN 978-1-61655-613-6
Volume 6	ISBN 978-1-61655-614-3
Volume 7	ISBN 978-1-61655-615-0
Legends	ISBN 978-1-50670-323-7

DARKHORSE.COM AVAILABLE AT YOUR LOCAL COMICS SHOP OR BOOKSTORE | TO FIND A COMICS SHOP IN YOUR AREA, CALL 1-888-266-4226

For more information or to order direct: • On the web: DarkHorse.com • Email: mailorder@darkhorse.com • Phone: 1-800-862-0052 Mon.–Fri. 9 AM to 5 PM Pacific Time.